# MORE IRISH SHORT STORIES

# More Irish Short Stories

## JOHN B. KEANE

THE MERCIER PRESS
DUBLIN and CORK

The Mercier Press Limited
4 Bridge Street, Cork
25 Lower Abbey Street, Dublin 1

© John B. Keane 1981

ISBN 0 85342 660 0

To My Friends
Phil and Mary Healy

*This book is published with the assistance of The Arts Council
(An Chomhairle Ealaíon).*

*The writer of this book was assisted by a contribution from The
Authors Royalty Scheme of The Arts Council (An Chomhairle
Ealaíon).*

Many of the stories in this book were originally published in
*The Limerick Leader, Cara, The Irish Press,* RTE and the
BBC.

*Printed by Litho Press Co., Midleton, Co. Cork.*

# Contents

# 1. Protocol

I could tell from the expression on Timmy Binn's face that he had come down from the hilltop on a special mission. Most times he called merely to pass away the winter nights. He would sit by the hearth with my uncle and his wife and maybe her father if the old man felt up to it. There they would exchange news and views until midnight when the party broke up after a cup or two of tea.

My uncle's house sat snugly in the lee of a small Sitka spruce plantation at the bottom of the hill whereas the Binn abode was almost at the top about a mile distant. At the time Timmy Binn was approaching his seventieth year which made him the youngest of three bachelor brothers and three spinster sisters who lived together in their ancient farmhouse which looked down on every other in the parish.

The isolation suited the Binns. They were seen in public by early morning mass-goers only. These, for the most part, would be old and retiring like themselves, venturing forth weekly to the village church in order to observe the Sabbath.

Timmy it was who did all the shopping. Every morning, Sunday included, he tackled the old black mare to the milk cart and guided her to the creamery with the tanks containing the daily yield from the twelve milch cows. When the milk was delivered he would purchase the necessary provisions and return home without further delay.

On Fridays he collected the several old age pensions due his brothers and sisters at the village post office.

Half of the money was spent on luxuries like coil tobacco, snuff and mixed fruit jam. The other half was credited to a joint account in a well worn post office book. This was left untouched over the years so that it might meet wake and funeral expenses when, one by one, the Binns would be faced with the ultimate contingency.

'Come up to the fire,' my uncle called as soon as the door was closed. Timmy's mouth opened to say something but he thought better of it and sat by the fire as instructed.

'You'll take a bottle of porter,' the uncle said. 'In fact,' said he before Timmy could answer, 'we'll all take a bottle of porter.' Normally Timmy Binn would have been offered tea but Christmas was not long past and there still remained some bottled porter after the festivities. The uncle uncorked three bottles. He handed one to Timmy and another to his father-in-law. The third he kept for himself. No glasses were used.

'Sláinte,' said the uncle as he lifted the bottle to his mouth.

'Sláinte,' the others answered and they did likewise. Each went halfway down and as soon as Timmy Binn had placed his on the floor at the side of his chair he readied himself to make an announcement. None came however. From where I sat reading at the kitchen table I could see that he was under great strain. He wanted to come out with something but couldn't. I was about to intervene and say 'Let Timmy talk', but I remembered that it was the custom to exhaust every other topic before asking for the reason behind any visit. I remembered that Timmy had arrived only a few weeks before on an errand for his sisters. He had spent nearly two hours talking in front of the hearth with my uncle and the old man. Finally when he was handed a cup of tea by the woman of the house he announced that he would not have time to drink it. He explained that he had been sitting in his own kitchen while his sisters were preparing supper when they suddenly discovered that there wasn't a grain of sugar in the house. Timmy had been dispatched straightaway for the loan of a cupful till morning. He nevertheless allowed himself to be coerced into drinking the tea on the grounds that his sisters would have gone ahead with the supper anyway in view of his long absence.

This time, however, an uncharacteristic agitation showed. He fussed and fidgeted but restrained himself, remembering that there was a ritual to be observed. Neither my uncle nor the old man commented on his restlessness. They presumed that he would withhold the reason for his visit as a matter of course until such time as he was asked. They knew quite well that he had come for a purpose other than sitting and talking but part of the proceedings consisted of endeavouring to deduce in their own minds precisely what that purpose was. The whole undertaking would be spoiled if he came out with his business straight-off. It mattered not how pressing that business might be nor did it count that he might be in a hurry back home. Tradition obliged him to sit it out until the proper time.

'There are poor people sheltering this night without a fire.' The old man of the house swallowed the remainder of his stout after he had spoken. He handed the empty bottle to my uncle in such a manner as to suggest that the opening of three more bottles might not be inappropriate.

'A good blaze is everything,' his daughter said, lovingly laying three large black sods on the perimeter of the fire, 'and I'll tell you what is more,' she went on, 'a good fire will draw pain out of a body.'

'Tuck, tuck,' her father said in agreement. The uncapped bottles were handed out again and the menfolk quaffed. A lengthy silence followed during which Timmy Binn stirred uneasily in his chair. My uncle and the old man exchanged knowing glances.

'We're on a big one this time,' the old man's expression spoke for him.

'No doubt about that,' Timmy's said. The silence continued. They were searching for clues, putting together bits and pieces of information from the happenings of the previous weeks. Something out of the ordinary had happened at Binn's, something not quite calamitous but yet important enough to make an easy-going hillman like Timmy Binn uneasy and fidgety.

'I mind worse winters nor this,' the old man spoke to relieve the tension.

'Tell us about the time of the big snow,' his daughter urged.

'I was only a boy then,' the old man began. We had heard the story twenty times but it was well suited to a winter's night and it always improved in the re-telling. Even Timmy Binn seemed to forget his assignment as the tale unfolded. All the while the wind howled in the chimney and now and then a shower of passing hailstones beat furiously on the windows. The narrative ended after a half hour with the old man declaring that he needed a drop of something stronger than common porter to restore his flagging energy.

'Story-telling is dry work.' This was a favourite

saying of his. Without a word his daughter removed herself and returned a moment later with a bottle of whiskey.

'I was keeping it for an occasion,' she explained, 'but I suppose this is as good an occasion as any.' She too sensed that Timmy was the bearer of exceptional tidings. The whiskey was her contribution to the pro-longment. A woman less sensitive to the lifestyle of the countryside might have terminated the programme there and then by simply doing nothing.

'Any sign of snow up your way, Timmy?' The uncle tendered the spirits and the question at the same time.

'The odd flake is all I've seen so far,' Timmy answered.

'The odd flake eh?' The old man pondered the response as he searched for further questions in his whiskey glass. Failing to find any he lifted it to his lips and skilfully tossed a dollop into his mouth where he allowed it to remain for a while before swallowing it with great relish. It provided him with the inspiration he needed. He was activated by an almost impercepti-ble spasm as the whiskey reached its destination. He nodded appreciatively.

'Right on target,' he said to nobody in particular. 'If the first shot hits the bullseye,' he declared, 'then all the other shots will do the same. It is vital, therefore, to hold the whiskey under your tongue until the stomach is ready to receive it. People don't know how to drink whiskey anymore. Nowadays they swallow it back like it was water and they're paralysed drunk before they know it.'

For a quarter hour he held forth on the subject of whiskey drinking. Whether it was the porter or the

11

whiskey or both, Timmy Binn had more or less resigned himself to the situation. He looked blankly into the fire as the old man roamed aimlessly over a wide field of topics. The uncle took over just as it seemed his father-in-law must topple into sleep from sheer verbal exhaustion. The uncle lacked the narrative skills of the old man but he, nevertheless, managed to contain the visitor with the sheer forcefulness of his dialogue. All the while the old man nodded drowsily but yet managed to stay awake. His daughter sat nearer to him so as to act as a prop whenever he leaned sideways. The uncle supported him on the other side.

Silently I went out of doors. The hail had stopped. The roadway had a bleached look. On the hilltop the Binn farmhouse was ablaze with light. I half expected to see one of the brothers descending the narrow roadway in search of Timmy but the hill road was empty. Undoubtedly there was something amiss at the top of the hill. Up until this time there had been but a single faint light to indicate the whereabouts of the Binn habitation. Now there was this unprecedented radiance shimmering outrageously in the lofty distance like a newly transfixed star of great magnitude. It outshone every other light in the countryside. Then a fleeting cloud obscured the moon and total darkness fell on the roadway. I hurried back to the house. Before going in I looked through the window into the kitchen. The old man's head drooped as he sat squeezed upright by his daughter and the uncle. She occupied herself with the darning of a sock nodding in assent at the observations being made by her husband. For his part he sat with flushed face and held forth for all he was worth using his long arms to stress the elements of his narrative that needed stressing. His mouth opened and closed with great rapidity. It seemed a grim tale indeed but it had little effect on the visitor.

Timmy Binn sat with his legs outstretched, his head forward on his chest as though he had been hypnotised, his empty glass cupped loosely in his grimy hand looking as if it must fall to the floor at any moment. Then the uncle suddenly finished his talk and twiddled his thumbs.

'What's the night like outside?' He asked the question as soon as I had reoccupied my chair.

'Black as pitch,' I answered.

'You won't get blacker than that.' This affirmation was addressed to Timmy Binn who emerged slowly out of his trance.

'What was that?' he asked apologetically.

'It don't matter,' the uncle reassured him.

'Anyone on the road?' the woman of the house enquired.

'Not a living Christian,' I answered, 'except that there is a fierce light on the hilltop.'

The lethargy which held sway for so long suddenly disappeared. Everybody was attentive.

'What part of the hill?' the uncle asked.

'Where Binn's is,' I answered, as casually as I could.

'Where Binn's is?' It was the old man coming into his own once more. This was the moment for which Timmy Binn had waited all night. Every eye was now turned upon him. His time had come at long last. A total of two and a half hours had passed since he first set foot in the kitchen. He placed his glass on the floor between his legs and folded his hands over his stomach waiting for the question that was to be his cue. It was posed by

13

the old man.

'And pray Timmy,' he said innocently, 'what business brought you down from the hill this night?'

'I would be wanting the loan of six or eight chairs,' said Timmy Binn.

'Why would you be wanting six or eight chairs?' It was the uncle's turn now.

'Because,' said Timmy Binn, 'one of us is dead and we're short of chairs for the wake.'

A brief silence ensued during which the uncle and the old man exchanged I-told-you-so glances. They had guessed right. They had been on a big one. The wait had been worthwhile and despite the importance of the mission due protocol had been observed. That was what really mattered.

# 2. Dousie O'Dea

If you were to ask anybody in the parish of Tanvally about Dousie O'Dea the answer would always be the same. She had no equal in the county when it came to the doing up of corpses. As she grew older she grew selective and practised her art on rare occasions only. Then there came an unhappy day when she announced that she was retiring altogether. Thereafter nothing could persuade her to continue. She declined even to indulge deathbed wishes.

It was in the little things that Dousie excelled. Where a wart dominated a certain area of the face when life throbbed in that face's temples there would be no sign in death that a wart ever existed. Hair that in life seemed lank and incapable of curling assumed, under Dousie's coiffeusage, a transfiguration so beauteous that seasoned corpse-viewers could only gasp upon beholding it. She had a special way with wrinkles. As she kneaded the ancient skin of pensioners these would vanish mysteriously one by one until the texture of the skin on the face of the subject assumed a girlish smoothness. Unsightly pimples were transformed into fetching beauty spots while minor distortions of the neck and ears were so skilfully adapted that they never failed to compliment the visage from which they once detracted.

Once and once only was her handiwork submitted for professional criticism. The cadaver in question was that of one Baldy Mullane, an aged agricultural labourer who suddenly made his farewell to this life while transplanting onions in a plot at the rear of his cottage. Dousie was called upon to ready him for his trip to the next world. This she did without fuss or delay. That night at Baldy Mullane's wake there was porter in abundance. Two half tierces were on tap. Wine and whiskey flowed freely. It had been Baldy's lifelong ambition to be waked decently. At the height of the mourning when the wake-room was crammed with sympathisers it was announced that an American holiday-maker by the name of Louis Blep had arrived for the dual purpose of paying his respects and inspecting the corpse. Blep was a small, fat, loquacious individual whose mother had been born and reared in Tanvally but was forced to emigrate to the United States in order to find employment. In Chicago she married a successful mortician of German extraction. His name was Ernst Blep. Louis was the sole outcome of the union. Ever since his Confirmation when his mother had first brought him on holiday to her parents' home in Tanvally Louis had paid regular visits to the maternal homestead. His mother and grandparents were long since dead but there was no scarcity of relations. He would spend a few days with each until his three weeks' holiday expired. Even if he had never heard of Dousie O'Dea's skills as an amateur mortician his presence would have been expected at the wake-house anyway.

He was greeted on arrival by Baldy Mullane's daughter, Bessie. A brimming glass of whiskey was thrust into his hand. He swallowed it neat at one go. This was the custom. He would be presented with a second glass as soon as he regained his breath after the first. This would be drunk at a more leisurely rate while he sympathised with the relations. As soon as he moved towards the wake-room door the occupants of the kitchen pressed forward. There were many who wanted to hear him confirm what they had long believed, that Dousie O'Dea was without peer when it came to the doing-up of corpses while others, a minority, hoped only that the visit would be a come-uppance for Dousie. Such is the price of fame and indeed in Tanvally as in other places there are always people who are incapable of saying a good word about anybody.

Preparatory to his entry Louis Blep handed his empty glass to Bessie Mullane. It would hardly have been in keeping with the occasion had he taken it into the wake-room. Handing it to Bessie was his guarantee that it would be filled upon his return to the kitchen. Louis hesitated for a moment at the wake-room door. He had already resolved to be uncritical of Dousie's efforts. Neither would he over-praise. A pleasant smile and a gentle nod of approval should keep everybody happy. He was quite unprepared for the eye-catching artistry which confronted him from the death bed. Baldy Mullane did not look a day over forty. His bald head glinted under the light of the sacred candles which stood in their pewter sticks at either side of the bed. The serenity of sanctity shone from his flawless face. If the expression thereon could have been translated into words it would have read: 'Gone straight to heaven. Signed Baldy Mullane.'

Louis knelt on one knee and whispered a hasty Lord's Prayer for the soul of the deceased. A number of sombrely dressed, elderly women sat on sugawn chairs at the other side of the bed. Their trained eyes missed nothing. If Louis Blep's inscrutable features were to register the most insignificant of changes it would be recorded at once and its character accurately interpreted. From time to time these frosty-faced fossils exchanged whispers, winks and nudges which spelt approval or disapproval of certain mourners. Otherwise they maintained a stony silence which helped immediately to chasten exuberant or drunken visitors. In fairness to them they helped to preserve the solemnity of the proceedings. Louis Blep rose and blessed himself, nodded respectfully in the direction of the vigilant elders and vacated the wake-room. A crowd gathered round him. He took momentary refuge in the full glass which Bessie Mullane handed him.

'Well?' A self-appointed spokesman for the group posed the question.

'I seen mugs in my time,' Louis Blep, having carefully considered the question, spoke from his heart, 'but I ain't never seen no mug like that in there. The guy's positively beautiful. This dame, what's her name?'

'Dousie O'Dea,' everybody chorused.

'She's a natcheral. If she was in the States with a talent like that she'd be a millionaire in no time.'

This put the seal on Dousie O'Dea's already prestigious reputation. Word of Louis Blep's commendation spread far and wide. From that night forth it was considered sacrilegious when unwittingly some innocent spoke disparagingly of Dousie. Her reputation was secure. That was why her retirement came as such a blow to those who had hoped for her ministrations at the end. Years passed but despite constant appeals she steadfastly refused to come out of retirement. As a result it greatly added to the respectability of a family if they could boast that one of their members had been done up by Dousie O'Dea. It was almost like owning a

Stradivarius. It carried with it more esteem than a marble headstone or a Celtic Cross and it wasn't that Dousie had lost her touch or that age had blunted her skill.

In her heart of hearts she knew that all her efforts, excellent and all as they were, had a sameness, an unchangeable texture, a sort of futile duplication. The cold truth was that no single one stood out above any other. No one would deny that they were all master-pieces and could not be bettered but was this enough? Should not there be one effort which crowned all the others? It was a niggling question and the older she got the more it vexed her. Hard as she tried she could not recall a particular corpse more pleasing to her than all the others. From her backward vantage point she had no way of knowing that the true artist can never be fully satisfied.

In time others came to take her place. She frequently viewed the end-products of her imitators. She had no choice. When neighbours died condolences had to be offered. This meant kneeling by the deathbed for as long as it took to intone a decade of the Rosary. She would have to be blind not to notice the bed's occupant. Always upon rising she would pass the same comment: 'A handsome corpse God bless her,' or if it was a man: 'A noble corpse God bless him.' She was con-ceding nothing. Everybody else said exactly the same thing. It was part of the ritual of all wake-house visits. Sometimes when her imitators excelled themselves the grim-faced custodians of the wake-room would alert themselves for Dousie's reaction. None save the customary comment was every forthcoming. Then on a hail-ridden, windy night in mid-January Dousie O'Dea had unexpected visitors. Her husband Jack it was who answered the timid knocking on the door. Jack and Dousie had not been blessed with issue. For all that they were well content with themselves and had no great wish for company other than their own.

'Who's out?' Jack O'Dea called.

''Tis only us,' came the response from outside.

'Yes,' said Jack O'Dea, 'but who is us?'

'Us is Thade and Donal Fizzell.' Jack recognised Thade Fizzell's booming voice.

'I declare to God!' Dousie spoke from her corner of the hearth, 'there is nothing so sure as that their sister Jule is dead.'

In the doorway the brothers shook the hailstones from their caps and shoulders.

'God bless all here.' They spoke in unison.

'Take off the coats and drive on up to the fire,' Dousie welcomed them as she rose to take their coats.

''Tis unmerciful weather entirely,' Thade Fizzell spoke to no one in particular.

'A coarse brush I wouldn't put out this night,' Donal, the smaller and younger of the pair spoke in support. When all were seated round the fire Dousie took a bottle and glasses from a well-concealed compartment high in the hearth wall. The bottle contained poitcheen. She poured until the brothers protested and then poured a extra dollop in case the protests were token. The brothers were well into their second glasses before conversation began in earnest. It touched first upon the vagaries of the winter weather, then upon the quality of fodder and potatoes until it centred upon the true purpose of the visit. The externals, however, had to be observed regardless of the importance of the news.

These outward flourishes helped to emphasise the main item which in this case happened to be, as Dousie had predicted, the recent demise of Jule Fizzell. The brothers were both in their early seventies which meant that Jule who was the oldest of the family could well be eighty years of age.

'Did she go quick the poor soul?' Dousie enquired after her death had been announced.

'Like that,' Thade Fizzell replied and flicked his fingers to indicate the speed of her departure.

'Darning socks she was in front of the fire when the needle tinkled on the hearthstone and the sock fell from her hand.'

'May God grant her a silver bed in heaven,' the aspiration came from Jack O'Dea.

'You know, of course,' Thade Fizzell cut short the celestial entreaties, 'she was anything but a handsome woman.'

The O'Deas nodded sympathetically and waited.

'In fact,' Thade continued, 'you'd be hard put to find uglier.'

'She was,' Donal Fizzell subscribed, 'the plainest creature I ever came across. I must say in truth, although she was my very own sister, that I used to keep a look-out in my travels for plainer but I looked in vain. Our Jule beat all I ever saw. That woman used to frighten the children on their way home from school. Even the crows avoided our haggard when she cocked her head in the air.'

When Donal finished Thade resumed.

'At dances long ago men used to talk sideways at the poor creature so as to avoid looking at her direct. In the end she gave up going to dances and contented herself

21

by her own hearth. Matchmakers came with accounts of likely men but one look was enough for them. What harm but she was as kind-hearted a soul as ever drew breath. There was a great heart cooped inside her breast and I never heard her cast a hard word on any creature living or dead.'

Thade Fizzell noted the tears that trickled down Dousie O'Dea's face. He nudged his brother. Donal maintained the advocacy. 'That dear soul,' he continued, 'wanted nothing only to see others happy but she did make one request. Every so often she would say, "There is something you boys must do for me." We never had to ask what it was. We knew it well enough from listening day in, day out. "When I'm stretched on my deathbed you'll bring Dousie O'Dea to do me up." It wasn't for the Pope of Rome she asked nor cardinals with their red hats. All she wanted was to be done up by Dousie O'Dea.'

A long, awkward silence followed. It was Jack O'Dea who broke it.

'Boys,' he said, 'Dousie is greatly honoured by all you say but what you ask is impossible.'

'Then let her tell us herself,' Thade Fizzell insisted. 'We are, at the very least, entitled to that.'

'It is as Jack says,' Dousie spoke with finality.

'With a face like Jule's,' Donal Fizzell said sadly, 'there is no hope she'll face for heaven. She'd be too ashamed. She'll most likely linger at the gate forever. I daresay it was too much to ask in the first place for there is no power on earth could transform our eyesore of a sister into a presentable corpse. It just cannot be done.'

'I did not say it could not be done,' Dousie cut in

pertly.

'Then you'll do it?' New hope radiated from Thade Fizzell's amiable face.

'I didn't say that either,' Dousie reminded him, 'but in view of all you have said and taking into account what your poor sister suffered in this world because of her looks I'll do her up for you, but it will be the last time these hands will ever decorate the dead.'

The brothers Fizzell could scarcely contain their delight. Old as they were they danced a jig on the flagstone of the hearth but stopped suddenly when Jack O'Dea reminded them that a sister of theirs lay dead. Dousie took immediate charge of the situation as soon as the brothers' rejoicing had fully subsided.

'Jack,' she said, 'you go straightaway and tackle the cob. You boys go on home and make arrangements for the wake. I'm going to the Room for to gather my accoutrements.'

At Fizzell's Dousie worked alone and in silence. She saw to it that the wake-room door was bolted from the inside. She had long determined that her craft, for what it was worth, would go to the grave with her. It had often been suggested that she adopt an apprentice or at least school some of the corpse-dressers who appeared after her retirement in the basics of the business. She had turned a deaf ear to such entreaties. She was well aware that any disclosure on her part would quickly erode the reverence in which she was held. Anyway it was her strongly held contention that corpse-dressers, like poets, were born, not made. Jule Fizzell proved to be the most difficult subject she had ever encountered. Luckily she had lost none of her old skill. Neither did her long lay-off impede the work in any way. An hour passed and then another. A voice from the kitchen asked if everything was alright. She replied in the affirmative and asked that there be no more such queries. She needed every last iota of her concentration for the job in hand. Indeed there were times when she despaired of effecting any change whatsoever, so complex and craggy were the features under her hands. Perspiration trickled down her face as the night wore on. Yet she persevered until slowly but surely a master-piece began to take shape. She became a trifle excited as she realised that this might well be the central gem in the wide brooch of her art. In the end, after nearly three hours of sustained effort, she had accomplished the impossible. She sat triumphantly on the bedside of her subject and for the first time in her life savoured the heady brew of total artistic satisfaction.

'That's not our sister,' were the first words uttered by Donal Fizzell. Thade simply stood transfixed. After a while he spoke.

'It's our sister alright,' he said, 'and it's what she might have been like if God had ordained it so.'

Jack O'Dea was aware from the moment his eyes met those of his wife that something extraordinary had taken place. When he surveyed the corpse he felt some of the ecstasy that she had felt. Before him on the bed lay one of the most beautiful women he had ever seen. The face that was once a travesty was now angelic, its sharp contours magically softened by the artistry of his wife. The Fizzell brothers had seated themselves on chairs, their unbelieving eyes firmly fixed on the ravish-ing creature on the deathbed. Now and then they would shake their heads or exchange mystified looks but no words came. The fact was that there were no words which would do proper justice to Dousie's creation. If there was a word that might be fittingly applied that word was alive for, in truth, Jule Fizzell had never looked more alive. In life men had looked the other way. In death they would look at Jule Fizzell a second time and remember her haunting beauty long after she had been claimed by the clay. After what seemed like hours the brothers stirred themselves from the trance which had mesmerised them. There was the wake to think of. The undertaker would have to be approached. Drink would need to be transported from the village. Victuals in plenty would have to be purchased, relatives notified and the hundred and one other items attended to, which all went into the making of a successful wake.

In the parish of Tanvally there are nights which are remembered above all others. There was, for instance, the night of the big wind and the night of Horan's last wren-dance. Of like calibre was the night of Jule Fizzell's wake. The mourners came from far and wide. Single, in pairs and in droves they came to view the Fizzell phenomenon. Those who had known her personally were awe-struck by the transformation. Those who came merely out of curiosity were lavish in their praise. None could recall a corpse possessed of so much charm and vivacity. The wake was a success from the outset. Instead of proving to be an embarrassment, as the brothers had feared, their departed sister had brought them honour and glory. They swaggered from kitchen to wake-room accepting sympathy and homage. Midway through the wake the drink supply ran dangerously low. A courier was quickly despatched to the village where the original order was repeated. It was delivered instantly. The publican in question was requested to be on hand should further supplies be needed. Thade and Donal Fizzell were determined to play their part in making the night a memorable one. Neighbours were commissioned to ensure that no glass remained empty for long. Pots of tea and plates of edibles were in constant circulation. By midnight the house was packed to suffocation. The sole topic of conversation was the corpse. She was showered with superlatives. Hardened reprobates whose previous wakeroom contributions rarely exceeded a single, mumbled prayer spent long periods on their knees, their eyes affixed to the deathbed whereon lay the loveliest creature they had ever beheld. There were many who revisited the wake-room several times. These consisted mainly of those who could not at first believe their eyes.

At one o'clock in the morning the drift homewards began. By four the house was deserted save for Thade and Donal Fizzell and a few cronies who elected to keep them company until daybreak. Having consumed their fill of drink the entire party lapsed into a drunken sleep around the fire. When they wakened in the morning the corpse had vanished. They looked under the bed but all they found there was a venerable chamber pot which had seen better days. They looked in the other rooms but found no trace of the missing cadaver.

While they had slept a strange thing had happened. In the Tanvally uplands, on a small isolated farm there resided a rough and ready sort of a fellow known far and wide as the Cowboy Cooney. No one knew for sure what his exact age might be. It was certain, however, that he was no chicken. He lived completely alone with neither chick nor child, wife nor parent. His only visitors were poitcheen dealers who came at monthly intervals to purchase his regular output of the precious brew. If, on rare occasions, other callers appeared on the narrow roadway which led to his house he made himself scarce in the hills and did not return till they had departed. From early afternoon he had been aware that something of importance had happened in the valley. As night came down and the lights of a hundred transports twinkled on the main road several miles below he grew alarmed.

'What can it mean?' he asked himself. Had there been an invasion of some kind? Had some unprecedented disaster struck the valley? He withdrew a poitcheen bottle from underneath the thatch and positioned himself on the pier of a gate the better to view the goings-on in the valley. Lights in their hundreds came and went. With over half the contents of the bottle safely tucked away the Cowboy decided that the activities down below merited his personal attention. He decided to bring the bottle with him for company. By the time he reached the Fizzel farmhouse which had seemed to him to be the nub of the bustle he saw only the sleeping figures by the fire. Cautiously he entered and surveyed the scene. On the table standing out from several empty contemporaries was a full bottle of whiskey. Since he had long since emptied his own bottle he put this welcome find to his head and downed at least two glasses in one long, single swallow. It was quite palatable although a lightweight concoction compared to his own home-made draughts. He sensed rather than saw that the cause of all the earlier comings and goings was to be found in the room so romantically flooded by flickering candle-light. He was not prepared for the sight which met his eyes. He stood with his mouth open for several moments utterly overcome by the radiant loveliness of the smiling lady who occupied the bed. It was this very smile which gave him the courage to advance a step or two. The Cowboy Cooney up until this moment had always been the very soul of shyness. This was no longer the case. The smile on the face of this wonderful woman on whom he had never before laid eyes had given him poise and confidence. He could see that she wished him to sit on the side of the bed. This he did and at once launched into the story of his life. He wept throughout the tragic aspects and the smile on her face seemed to change to one of sympathy. Emboldened by her obvious fondness for him he took her hand not noticing the coldness.

'Will you marry me?' he asked.

At this she merely smiled but he could see that it was a smile of content. What a placid, sensitive, modest creature she was.

'Then you'll be mine?' he asked. Again the affirming smile.

'There is no need to speak,' he told her, 'your smile has spoken for you.' Gently he lifted her into his arms and staggered into the kitchen where he addressed the sleeping inmates.

'I am taking this woman to be my lawful wedded wife,' he announced. 'If any man here has anything to say let him speak now or forever hold his peace.'

He waited for a reply and was rewarded with an assortment of drunken snores which he took to mean approval. Triumphantly he blundered into the night. Next morning they were discovered by a group of schoolchildren. Jule Fizzell was cradled in the arms of the Cowboy Cooney. The serene smile on his face was matched only by that on the face of the corpse. He snored blissfully. She made no sound at all.

When, later in the day, the news was relayed to Dousie O'Dea she smiled to herself. She had reached the final pinnacle. Her life's work was complete. For one man she had brought the dead to life. For this, in itself, she would be remembered beyond the grave.

# 3. Thrift

It was his father's miserliness that killed John Cutler.
That's what the neighbours said afterwards. That was
what Mick Kelly the postman said and Mick knew the
Cutlers better than anybody. His cottage stood at the
entrance to their farm. When John Cutler reached his
thirty-fifth year he confronted his father with the fact
that he was at the halfway stage in his life's span with
nothing to show for it.

'A few more years,' he complained, 'and I'll be an
old man.'

His father nodded but did not otherwise commit himself.

'I have a notion of getting married.' He threw the
bait out hopefully but the older man refused to rise to
it.

While John stood waiting for some expression of
sympathy or approval his mother entered the kitchen.
At once she sensed there was a showdown in progress.
She busied herself by the fireplace silently praying that
her industry would exempt her from taking sides.

'What do you expect me to do?' Tom Cutler rose
from his chair and went to the open door where he
absently surveyed the distant hills.

'You could sign over the place,' John suggested.

'Can't do that. Damn well you know I can't do that.'

'But why not?'

'Why not he asks and he knowing well. What's to
become of your mother and me if you bring another
woman in here?'

'Ye can have a room.'

'A room eh! A whole room to ourselves! And what about our feeding and a bit of money?'

'There will be guarantees in the agreement. The solicitor will see to that.'

'And will the solicitor be here every day to see that the guarantees are carried out? There is no way I would allow another woman in here without five thousand pounds. I'd also want a separate dwelling on the land, nothing fancy, mind you, just a simple cot for two. That's not asking a lot now is it?'

John threw his hands upwards in a gesture of total despair.

'Where would I get five thousand pounds,' he cried out angrily, 'and the money to build a house?'

'If your future wife had a fortune it would help.'

'My future wife as you call her has no money.'

'You could borrow,' the old man said.

'I couldn't,' John told him, 'not that kind of money; a few thousand yes but not what you ask.' Tom Cutler shrugged his shoulders. 'It's tough,' he said, 'but I have to think of myself and your mother. If I don't nobody else will. That's been proved a thousand times over. Now if you've finished you might go down and turn in the cows.'

'So that's to be the end of it is it? My future is on the line and you want me to turn in the cows. Have you no more to say to me?'

'What more is there to say except that you have yourself to thank for the way you are today.'

'Myself to thank!' the words exploded from John's mouth.

'Oh now face up to the truth my boy. You didn't miss a night in the pub these last fifteen years.'

31

'Oh come off it,' John shouted. 'A few pints was the most I ever had and the beggars on the road had that.'

'A few pints every night,' his father pointed out, 'is a lot of pints come the end of the week. A thrifty man would have a nice pile put by at this time of his life.'

'What could I put by out of the miserable few pounds you paid me? After a packet of cigarettes and a drink there was nothing left. Nothing.' He spat out the words and brushed by his father with clenched fists.

'Drink and cigarettes, sure recipes for poverty,' the old man flung the words after him like stones after a worthless hound. He stood silently for a long while in the doorway. Then he turned to his wife.

'What do you make of that?' he asked. They were a wizened pair, looking older by far than their years. Both had sallow, pinched faces, stooped frames and decaying teeth. They presented an overall picture of neglect and want.

'I don't know what to say,' Minnie Cutler responded.

Tom shook his head at the outrageousness of it all.

'Do you think he has a woman itself?' he asked.

'I don't think so,' she answered after a while, 'least-ways not a regular one.'

'I thought as much. All he wants is to get his hands on the place and then drink it out.'

'Maybe if you were to give it over to him he'd come by a woman. No one will take with him unless the place is his own.'

'I can't do that. We both know it won't work.'

'But we have enough Tom. God knows how much you have in the banks.'

'You couldn't have enough for this world you foolish woman. When I go the place will be his but till that time

32

he'll draw his wage and dance to my tune. I broke my back for this place and so did you. He'll bide his time.'

'I don't know Tom.' Minnie Cutler folded her arms. 'He's thirty-five. He's going to seed. Most men of his age have their own places or at least they have the handling of the money.'

'It won't work Minnie,' Tom Cutler was adamant. 'Look around you. Look what happened to them that signed over.'

'Some have it good Tom.'

'God's sake woman will you not be codding yourself. They're only letting on to have it good. Most of them are prisoners in the homes they once owned.'

'But isn't that the whole cause of the trouble Tom? Those that bought houses in the town or rented rooms are content enough. It's only when you have two women under the one roof that the trouble starts.'

'Do you want me to spend every penny I possess on a house. Is that it?'

'It needn't be big.'

'Of course it needn't be big but the money will be big and we'll end up paupers depending on a daughter-in-law for handouts.'

'If you signed over we'd have our old age pensions.'

'Will you get it into your head woman that I will not sign over. Do you think I'm mad. You want me to part with all I have in this world with one stroke of a pen.'

'You could go halves with him.'

'Won't work. The place isn't big enough to support two families.'

'Would you not tell him that you'd be prepared to sign over after a year or two?'

'No I would not, nor after twenty years if I live that

long. There's a bit of a want in that fellow. He's a man for the good times. All he wants is drink and fags and carousing.'

'Still he's a good worker.'

'Is he now and pray how do you think he'd fare without me managing the place?'

'A woman would manage it for him quick enough.'

'This places calls for a thrifty man, a man that won't squander money foolishly. Let him wait. He'll appreciate it all the more when 'tis his. I'm away to the cows.'

'Who's to say but you're right,' Minnie Cutler conceded. Experience had taught her that it was prudent to concede ground which she knew she could not win anyway. Consequently there was never conflict between them, at least not of late.

For years too she had not mentioned his tight-fistedness. She took it for granted. According to him there was never anything to spare for clothes or holidays or titbits. He would always provide enough for the bare necessities but nothing more. In time she had stopped asking. It made for a peaceful atmosphere and in her estimation that was worth all the deprivation. Waste not want not had been Tom Cutler's strategy from the day he assumed ownership of the farm. It had been heavily in debt. Minnie's modest fortune had not been enough to compensate but non-stop penny-pinching had. Now they had cash in the bank and the land was stocked to its capacity. As the money mounted Tom would regularly repeat a phrase which he had coined the day he discovered he was out of the red. 'Thrift won't lose,' he would say, 'because thrift can't lose.' The logic of his composition appealed more and more to him as the years went by.

He was well aware that his neighbours and those who knew him further afield criticised him constantly for what he considered to be one of the great virtues. His parsimony had become something of a local joke. Those who conducted church gate collections for various charities would nudge each other when Tom Culter approached. He never subscribed no matter how worthy the cause. As soon as he had passed the collection tables he would permit himself the faintest of smiles. He smiled purely and simply because he still had his money. That, to Tom Cutler, was a genuine cause for mirth. He really relished such incidents. They were the only luxuries in which he indulged.

His son John, on the other hand, was known as a decent type. He hadn't much, his neighbours said, but by God that much was yours if you wanted it.

'He didn't bring it from his father,' Mick Kelly would say, ''tis from the grandfather he brought it, his father's father. Now there was your decent man. Give you the shirt off his back he would.'

Inevitably these assessments of his son would be relayed back one way or another to Tom. They occasioned him many a smile. So John was like his grandfather, was he, the same grandfather who drank himself to death and mortgaged the farm up to the hilt, the same grandfather who couldn't call on a shilling to bury the wife who died prematurely from shame. Tom had been forced to surrender the few pounds he had saved through his teens to buy a cheap coffin and have High Mass said for his mother. It had been a bitter lesson. His father had shamed him into putting up the money. He resolved immediately after his mother's funeral that his financial standing would never be revealed to anybody again, not even to his wife. Oh she knew he had money and she might guess rightly that it was a tidy bit but in this respect she would be close-mouthed because no matter how much she might crave after a commodity her need for security outweighed all else. From the start she had wanted him to part with his money. First the curtains hadn't been good enough, then the furniture, then the wallpaper and inevitably the house itself. He had always heard her out patiently. He would put her off with promises but as the years passed and he began to accumulate a little money he was able to boast that his frugality was paying off. In time she began to see that he had been right.

'Wouldn't we be in a nice way now,' he often told her, 'if I had given in.'

He had another son Willie, a subcontractor in England. A thrifty man was Willie. On the day of his departure Tom had handed him his fare and a ten pound note.

'If you have any sense,' he warned him, 'you'll not break that note needlessly. Put it aside and soon you'll have another to keep it company.'

And how much had Willie today? Willie had plenty because he had listened. More important nobody but Willie himself knew how much Willie had. That was the trouble about possessing money. You might spend years saving it while your very own kin had no thought but to squander it while you'd say Jack Robinson.

John Cutler's attitude towards his parents changed dramatically after the confrontation. It had been his wont each night upon returning home from the pub to impart the latest gossip going the rounds and to give an account of the activities of the pub's patrons if such

MORE IRISH SHORT STORIES

activities warranted it. His parents looked forward to this nightly report, especially his father although he never commented, whatever the content. He enjoyed it all the more because it cost nothing. They would have retired before his arrival but the bedroom door would be partly open in expectation.

Now there was no communication between them. Tom and Minnie were not unduly worried. He had sulked before but had come out of it after a few days. This time it was to be different. Weeks went by and then months until Tom closed the bedroom door to show that he didn't care. Around this time John started to grow careless about his appearance. Frequently too he came home drunk from the pub. Some mornings he was unable to rise for the milking. Minnie grew worried when she overheard him talking in his room. She relayed the news to Tom who put it down to drink.

'Wasn't I the wise man,' he told her, 'to hold on to what I had. Wouldn't we be in a nice way now depending on a drunkard.'

The rift became worse when John demanded an increase in wages.

'What do you want it for?' his father had asked curtly.

'I need it to keep pace,' John answered patiently.

'To keep pace with what, the price of drink is it?'

'There's more than drink gone up and well you know it. I need a new suit and a few shirts. My best shoes are beyond repair.'

'Wait till the fall of the year,' had been Tom Cutler's response. 'I'll know better where I stand.'

'And the rise?'

'I don't see what you need a rise for unless 'tis drink.'

The old man had gone to the bedroom and locked

37

himself in to avoid further argument. In despair John went straight to the pub where he stayed till midnight. When he came home he tried to open the bedroom door but it was still locked. They could hear him in the kitchen talking to himself. Neither said a word for a long while. Finally Minnie broke the silence. She spoke in a whisper not wishing her voice to carry.

'Would it not be better to relent a little?' she suggested.

'No.' Tom's reply was emphatic.

'But he's acting so queerly.'

'You want me to give in to a madman is that it?'

'No, no, that's not it at all. All I want is for you to make a concession.'

'I'll make no concession to drink woman and that is that. Now go to sleep.'

Minnie Cutler sighed. After a while she spoke for the last time before falling asleep.

'Who's to say but you're right,' she said.

The following evening Mick Kelly the postman called. He came in his Sunday clothes. The old folk welcomed him. There was no sign of John.

'Sit down, sit down.' Tom Cutler pulled a chair from under the table and placed it near the fire.

'And how's herself?' Minnie Cutler asked.

'Never better missus thank you,' Mick Kelly replied cheerfully.

In any other house in the neighbourhood he would have been royally received. The whiskey bottle would have appeared. The kettle would have been put down to boil. Minnie who was never embarrased by similar situations fumbled for words on this occasion but could find none. Mick Kelly was a good neighbour. For once she would have liked to offer him something. Her husband read her thoughts.

'I daresay you've had your supper Mick,' he said with forced joviality.

'Just after rising from the table,' came the ready-made answer.

'You're welcome to eat, you know that,' Minnie spoke half-heartedly.

'Oh I know that missus,' came the reassuring reply, 'I know that well.'

He made it sound convincing to put Minnie at her ease. He could not recall ever having received as much as a mouthful of tea at Cutler's. Neither could anybody else. Even the beggars of the roadway gave the place a wide berth. Some said there were barely visible scratches on the gate piers down by the main road, the secret sign language of the tinker folk: 'Pass by' the scratches said or so it was believed.

For an hour or more the three spoke of weather, crops and cattle, then of the neighbours and lastly of the great wide world. The ancient Stanley range had grown cold for want of fuelling. There were a few embers buried in the ashes but to stoke the firebox would be to despatch its entire contents into the ashpan beneath. Mick Kelly knew that it would be unthinkable for the Cutlers to replenish the fire so late in the evening.

'Well,' said he and he rose from his chair, 'I'll have to be going but before I do I had better bring out what brought me.' He cleared his throat and rubbed his large hands together, this to intimate that his mission was a delicate one.

'I've come about John,' he said. 'You may tell me it's

39

none of my business but I have known the three of you all my life and I feel I have earned the right to bring this matter to your notice.' Here he paused waiting for word to proceed.

'What is it about John?' Tom Cutler asked.

'He's not himself these days,' Mick Kelly answered. 'He's drinking too much and he's in debt poor fellow. It's not a lot, a few pounds here and there. He owes myself a tenner but that's not why I'm here and I'd gladly forget it if I thought it would help the man.

'Let him stop drinking and he'll soon have his debts paid,' Tom cut in.

'I'm afraid,' Mick Kelly spoke ruefully, 'most of the drink comes from people who are sorry for him.'

'He's turned into a bum then has he?'

'No. That isn't so at all. Most people will throw a drink a fellow's way if they think he has a problem. It's their way of sympathising.'

'What do you want me to do?'

'Rise his wage for a start. Give the poor fellow a few hundred to pay his debts. That's all. I promise you won't know the man after.'

'I'll tell you something now Mick Kelly and I'll tell you no more.' Tom Cutler rose and faced him. He moistened his thin lips before he spoke. 'When I took over here there was a crippling debt. I was advised to sell but I stuck it out whatever. It took the best years of my life to pay back the money my father squandered. It was a terrible burden for a young man and now when I'm old you want me to pay my son's debts as well. Is that to be the story of my life, to pay back the debts of two drunkards, my father and my son?'

'I can't counsel you further Tom,' Mike Kelly said

quietly. 'I can only tell you that all is not well with your son.'

'It's not my doing Mick.'

'I didn't say it was Tom. The poor fellow is demented and what harm but he could have enough if he wanted but he's too bloody honest.'

'I don't follow you,' Tom Cutler frowned.

'He could be selling the odd bag of corn behind your back and he could be transferring a gallon or two of milk to a crony. There's a lot doing it and getting away with it but not John Cutler. He could be lifting the occasional bag of spuds.'

Tom Cutler stamped the concrete floor with his right foot. 'He could in his eye,' he whipped back. 'If there was a grain of corn taken, or a single spud or a solitary pint of milk I'd know about it. He knows that. You know that and I know that and that's the reason he hasn't lifted anything so far. His first time would be his last time. I have another son, remember, a man who wouldn't be long answering my call if I sent for him.'

'I beg of you Tom not to renege on John.' Mick Kelly's appeal was fervent.

'I never reneged on him. He had cattle of his own remember. He drank the proceeds every time.'

'And I tell you he drank no more than anybody else,' Mick Kelly stuck to his purpose.

'I'm tired, Mick.' Tom Cutler returned to his chair. He was making it clear that as far as he was concerned the discussion was closed. Mick Kelly looked from husband to wife. For a moment he considered making a final appeal but thought better of it. The eyes of both were now focused on the ashpan of the Stanley. They leaned forward on their chairs the better to gaze upon it. As well as dismissing him the pose also suggested a show of solidarity.

'Goodnight,' Mick Kelly threw back as he opened the kitchen door.

'Goodnight Mick,' they spoke in unison without averting their heads. Mick Kelly felt as if he had closed the door on a tomb. He hurried home to his wife. He had promised to tell her how he fared before going to the pub.

As soon as the fall of the year had established itself John Cutler laid it on the line for the old man.

'I need decking out from head to toes,' he said, 'and it cannot be put off any longer. You will also double the money you are paying me now. Nothing less will do. Any farmer in the neighbourhood would do better by me.'

'Let me think about that one for a while,' Tom Cutler had told him. 'The fall isn't full out yet you know,'

It was the way the old man had said it that nettled John. It was as though he had made some outrageously childish claim and had not been taken seriously, had been humorously rebuffed. Was his father playing for time and if so why? The old fellow had been acting too independently of late, not caring whether John rose or slept it out in the mornings, whistling to himself and walking off whenever John grumbled about his lot. It was a totally new and inexplicable phase in their relationship. Had the old man something up his sleeve? John grew moodier as the autumn drew to a close. He was no longer asked to go to the village for farm or household necessities. He suspected he was being subtly isolated. Whenever he entered the kitchen they busied themselves ostentatiously with needless chores or if they were engaged in conversation it was immediately terminated when he put in an appearance. It was as though his father wished him to know that he had better tread warily, that there might be more strings to his bow than were apparent. There could only be one answer. They had contacted Willie with a view to bringing him home but how to be sure, how to make certain? Mick Kelly would know.

'It's a question I am not at liberty to answer,' Mick Kelly told him firmly when John Cutler demanded to know if there had been any exchange of letters between his father and Willie.

'Then there is!' John banged his pint glass triumphantly on the bar counter.

'No,' Mick assured him, 'there's isn't. Take my word for it. You have nothing to worry about from that quarter, at least as far as I know.'

John shook his head glumly. 'He has some ace in the hole,' he said, 'it has to be Willie.'

The Cutlers did not possess a motor car. The only concession Tom Cutler had made to modernisation was to invest in a second-hand tractor and he did this reluctantly. Until the arrival of the tractor he depended on a pair of horses. He greatly deprecated the disposal of these but compensated himself with the purchase of a pony. He refused to buy a motor car. He had a light cart made for the pony and used it to convey himself and Minnie to Mass, for occasional trips to the village and for work in the bog during the turf harvesting. The tractor with a trailor attached was used chiefly for conveying the milk to the village creamery and for general farm work although John used it regularly to get to and from the pub.

As they breakfasted one morning towards the end of September the old man addressed his wife.

'As soon as you've finished the washing-up,' he informed her, 'I'll tackle the pony for you. There's a few items to be got from the village.'

Minnie nodded obediently.

'You'll take him handy,' Tom said, 'as the reins is that bit wore.'

Again Minnie nodded.

'You'll bring the usual groceries, a quarter pound of three inch nails and eight yards of rope. 'Tis time the turf was drawn out. The laths on the rail need securing and a new reins will be wanted.'

Again Minnie nodded dutifully. 'Will that be all?' she asked.

'That will be all,' Tom Cutler said.

'Bring a handful of fags as well will you?' John added.

The old couple exchanged looks but no comment was forthcoming. Tom arose and went towards the door. Before going out he turned.

'You will bring back the items I ordered,' he said, 'and no more.' Hands in pockets he went whistling into the sunlight. Without a word John rose and followed. His mother would have restrained him but he was gone before she could speak. What she wanted to tell him was that she would bring a few packets of cigarettes unknown to his father but the words just wouldn't come out. She had been frightened by the look on John's face as he left. At first she feared that he would waylay his father and have it out with him but no, he had gone straight to the tractor, started it and driven off. Mick Kelly's words came back to her.

'I can't counsel you further,' he had said. 'I can only tell you that all is not well with your son.'

From force of habit she refused to ponder on the problem, concentrating instead on the trip to the village. She sensed, however, that events were coming to a head. Her intuition told her that something would have to be done if a calamity were to be avoided. There was no point in bringing the matter up with her husband. She had tried repeatedly since Mick Kelly's visit but he had smothered every effort at the outset. She resorted to the only means of succour remaining to her. Rummaging in her apron pocket she withdrew her Rosary beads and silently began the long count of Hail Marys. She would pray the whole way to and from the village and she would light candles in the parish church. The thought consoled her. The peace and beauty of the candle altar would be a tonic in itself, the very thing to bring her out of herself. She was unaccustomed to such treats. As she led the pony towards the roadway there was a lightness in her step that she hadn't experienced for months. In the village she saw a tractor which looked like John's outside one of the public houses but her new found elation was such that she felt able to ignore the implications involved. In the church she would find refuge from all embarrassments. There was no doubt in her mind about that and was not this as it should be? Was it not her entitlement?

Mick Kelly dismounted from his motor cycle at the entrance to the Cutler farm. He didn't have a letter but he had resolved to face up to Tom Cutler a second time. The day before he had encountered Minnie on her way from the village but she had not reined up to talk. Neither had she returned his salute. He had noticed the beads entwined about her fingers. He had remounted then and gone about his business. He had planned a new approach for this second appeal. This time he would draw Minnie into the thick of things whether she wished it or not. He believed that deep down she sympathised with John and he would be depending on this. It would be to his advantage if she were alone when he arrived but failing that he would involve her anyway. As he neared the house he sensed there was something wrong, something disproportionate. There was a new and terrible dimension to the area left of the house where the last leaves on a stand of ash trees whispered in the morning wind. There was an ominous addition to the familiar landscape and yet, though he was curious, he could not bring himself to look. This, however, could be that he already knew the awful nature of the intrusion. Slowly he forced his eyes to the left, eyes that started to fill with terror the moment he decided to confirm his worst fears. What he saw before him was the ultimate in physical distortion. The body of John Cutler hung from a stout branch extending from one of the ash trees. Around his neck was the shining new rope his mother had purchased in the village the day before. He was barefoot. His shoes had fallen to the ground. They lay directly beneath his feet. Mick Kelly made the sign of the cross and threw the cycle to one side. His next reaction was to pound the kitchen door. Instead he drew a deep breath and knocked gently. The door opened at once by Tom Cutler.

'I have bad news.' Mick Kelly bent his head to avoid the rheumy eyes. Tom Cutler made his task easy.

'I know,' he said, 'I was just going for help.'

He had, he explained, been changing into a fresh shirt. His shortcoat lay in readiness on the table. Minnie sat soundlessly by the Stanley, her beads clutched in her hands, her body rocking forward and backwards on the chair. All the time her lips moved in prayer.

'Will you take him down?' Tom Cutler asked.

'Yes, of course,' Mick answered, surprised by the old man's matter-of-factness. Despite the shock which he must have undergone he seemed to be his everyday self.

'You'll need a ladder,' Tom Cutler said.

'And a knife,' Mick enjoined.

'What do you want with a knife?' Tom asked.

'To cut the rope,' Mick responded.

'A saw is what you want,' Tom reminded him. 'A saw to cut the branch.'

Mick listened with growing wonder as the old man explained.

'A branch can be had for nothing,' he said, 'a rope costs money. Besides 'tis wanted for a reins.'

Buttoning his shortcoat he led the way to a small out-house. He emerged with a short ladder which he handed to Mick. He re-entered the house and emerged with a rusty saw. He motioned a bemused Mick Kelly to follow him towards the ash grove. Overhead the dry leaves flickered around his dead son. Some fell to the ground to join the others already rotting there.

47

# 4. Under the Sycamore Tree

Jimmy Bowen was by no means fastidious, yet every evening he would shave and wash meticulously before donning his best clothes in preparation for his trip to the river side. Having left the house he would stand in front of the shop window and take careful stock of himself. Should there be the slightest evidence of disorder anywhere on his person he would re-enter the house straightaway and set about correcting the imperfection. Having satisfied himself that every possible step had been taken regarding the re-organisation of his appearance he would present himself a second time to the shop window. Often he would stand there for several minutes pretending to be engrossed in a study of the window's contents whereas he was really searching for flaws in his appearance. When he was satisfied that no further improvement could be effected he would set off on his walk. The time he chose varied from season to season but always it would be roughly a half hour before darkness fell. First he would stroll leisurely through the streets before arriving at the laneway which led to the river side path. The moment he sighted the water his features underwent a change. His eyes grew brighter. His ears seemed to prick as though he were alerting himself for an exciting encounter. He became a different person.

At sixty Jimmy Bowen was a spare, grey-haired, lively man who moved with an athlete's facility. He was well off. Rumour had it that he never married because the girl he loved was killed in a car accident or drowned or worse. Nobody was quite clear. He had left the town in his late teens and returned twenty years later to take over the family hardware business when his father was taken ill. He had never seen eye to eye with the old man although they had never lost touch or so it was said. When the elder Bowen died Jimmy assumed control. His mother passed on shortly afterwards and it seemed inevitable that he would take a wife. He was young enough. A fit man of forty with his reputed means should have no trouble. He remained single, however, and was the bane of the town's over-blossomed spinsters for several years. At sixty with his hair whitened by the years he was no longer regarded as a candidate for the marriage stakes. His business prospered and there was much conjecture as to what would happen when he grew too old to carry on. He had a first cousin in a distant town, a ne'er-do-well with a large brood. Jimmy was persuaded by friends of the family that it would be an act of charity to bring the oldest boy into the business. It hadn't worked. The lad knew it all from the outset. He disappeared one day with several hundred pounds and was heard of no more.

The river side path which was the route of Jimmy's evening strolls was flanked on the one side by giant oaks and sycamores and on the other by the wide sweep of the river bank. It was a picturesque walk less frequented now than at any time in its history. Lovers no longer dallied there, preferring to speed through the countryside in motor cars. Older people, unless the weather was exceptionally fine, chose to sit and watch television. Consequently the only people Jimmy Bowen met were the occasional fowler and fisherman. This was the way he liked it even though it must be said that he entertained other secret aspirations. His favourite time was when darkness descended. To celebrate this delicate event he would stand unmoving under a favourite sycamore. It was best when no breezes blew. On these occasions of tranquility he would stand entranced, utterly absorbed by what was happening. Sometimes the motionless lineaments of the river would be mottled with infinitesimal flecks of foam. Even the birds would be hushed. It would be that precise time of evening when light resigns itself to half-light yielding finally to darkness and it seemed all nature was aware that consummate stillness was required if an honourable surrender were to take place. This was the very time when Jimmy Bowen longed for fulfilment of his secret aspirations. Quite simply what he hoped for was that a woman, the woman of his dreams, might emerge from the river side shadows and stand by his side to share in the romantic transition. It was, he knew, more than he was entitled to expect in such a place and at such a time. When as always she failed to materialise he would return the way he had come still cherishing the notion that she might appear before him out of one of the many bowers and groves along the way. At the back of his mind was the certainty that she would appear one evening. She would just happen to be there and that would be that. When it happened he would take her hand and they would return together towards the lights of the town. Words would be unnecessary.

The cold truth was that for twenty years Jimmy had returned to the town empty-handed but this had not succeeded in putting a damper on his expectations. He was as hopeful as ever. In the shop he worked with such earnest endeavour that no onlooker could possibly credit that the man's private life was founded on such improbable romantic notions. The very opposite would seem to be far more likely. His staff consisted of two counterhands, middle-aged brothers who had started their apprenticeships with his father. There was a general factotum, an elderly fellow, another relict from his father's tenure and there was Miss Miller. It would be difficult to determine Miss Miller's exact age. Mousy Miller the customers called her. She had joined the staff at the time of his father's illness and spent her working hours in an elevated glass office where she could command a view of every corner of the shop. She dressed chastely, wore spectacles and rarely used make-up. She had few friends and seemed content to spend most of her free time with her landlady, an elderly widow. Originally she hailed from the midlands. Her people, it was believed, were modest farmers. Jimmy rarely entered the office. When he did it was at Miss Miller's invitation. She always stood when he entered and allowed him to take the seat which she had just vacated. Usually the visit would consist of inspecting a contractor's account which might have exceeded the stipulated limit or to discuss the necessity for consulting a solicitor over other unpaid accounts of long standing. She always called him Mister Bowen. He never called her anything but Miss Miller. Although he never objected to these occasional conferences he always felt that his presence was superfluous. She might appear to be mousy and effete but her knowledge of the business was astonishingly comprehensive. The books were immaculately kept. At a moment's notice she could provide an exact rundown of the firm's financial standing for any period. It was she who dealt with the auditors, saw to the stocktaking and staff bonuses, made up the weekly wage packets and took on the hundred and one other minor tasks which contributed to the running of a successful business. It could be said that she knew her employer inside out. Jimmy knew her worth and paid her accordingly. Ask anywhere in the town and you would be told that, whatever else, Jimmy Bowen was first and foremost a decent man.

He had a somewhat different relationship with the rest of the staff. A casual customer would be hard put to know who was boss and who was counterhand. It worked well. The country people who patronised the shop liked a man without pretension, a man who would sit on the counter and pass the time of day. He had other traits which appealed to townspeople and country people alike. The chief of these was his tendency to take off on the occasional skite. He never took a conventional holiday. When the urge caught him, an urge which generally coincided with a fine spell, he would betake himself to the office pay slot and indicate his financial requirements to Miss Miller.

'Slip us a few hundred,' he might say. The money, in fivers and tenners, would be forthcoming at once without comment of any kind from Miss Miller.

'See you in a few days,' he would say as soon as the notes were pocketed. Home then to change into slacks, pullover and sandals. Garage next for a petrol fill and a hasty check of elementals. Thence to the nearest city or if the season were right to a distant holiday resort. His customers received news of these breaks with amusement. They knew the drill or thought they did. There had to be a woman or women. Why else would he go on his own? A good man's case this. Not even a step-mother would blame him. Many envied him the manner in which he took off in the first place. He needed nobody's permission and best of all he could come back when it suited him. On his return he never tendered the least information as to how he had fared, a sure sign, this his friends said, that a debauch had taken place.

The truth was that Jimmy Bowen did no more than sleep out in the mornings. The remainder of the day he spent inspecting the neighbourhood pubs and hotels. Sometimes he drank on his own. Other times he joined up with single gentlemen like himself or became involved in sing-songs. By midnight it would be as much as he could do to locate his room under his own steam. This then was the pattern of his respite. There had never been any serious involvement with a woman. He remained faithful to his river side fantasies and would fall into a happy if drunken sleep recalling the enchanting images of his favourite place or endeavouring to trace the shadowy features of the lovely creature who had thus far failed to realise herself from the place in question. Always he slept soundly, not waking till the chambermaids knocked on his door at a time when the morning was well advanced. He never surfaced before noon. By the time he had read through the morning papers lunch would have become available. Having partaken he would sit for a while before indulging in the only physical exercise of the day. This consisted of an hour long stroll after which he felt free to indulge himself in the first drink of the day. After a sojourn of four to five days his appetite for change would be sated and he would return home. There would be no drink on the day of the homecoming. He also made a point of arriving at the shop after dark. After a snack he would make straight for his bed where he stayed until the effects of the prolonged booze had worn off. As a rule this took no more than a sleep out until the late afternoon of the following day when he would arise refreshed and ready to resume his normal way of life. This was not to say that he was abstemious between skites. Most nights after returning from the river he stopped off at the Anglers' Rest where he allowed himself a whiskey or two before polishing off a few pints of draught stout. He never drank alone. There was always a crony or two in attendance and invariably he joined up with these until time was called.

Shortly after his sixtieth birthday he embarked upon the longest and most intensive skite of his career. He departed the town early on Monday afternoon and was not seen again in its vicinity for a period of ten days. What transpired during that time will never be fully revealed. Even with the aid of Miss Miller, if Jimmy Bowen ever endeavoured to itemise the events which took place, the task would be impossible for the excellent reason that they were beyond recall. To be more accurate it could be said that they had foundered irrevocably in an alcoholic haze. Occasionally in later years glimpses of that foggy interlude would be borne back to him but none of sufficient duration or clarity to enlighten him. It was, as he intimated to his cronies not long after his return, the father and mother of all skites, and the cronies to give them their due accepted this evaluation without question. Jimmy Bowen was not a man to exaggerate. There was no doubt that he had been on the skite of a lifetime. What he did remember, most vividly at that, was waking up on the final day. His head throbbed with a pain so overpowering that he despaired of ever facing the world again. For hours he tossed and turned on the bed. Towards late afternoon he steeled himself with every ounce of resolve at his disposal and entered the bathroom. He filled the bath with cold water and stood nearby in his pelt waiting for it to fill. This will kill me or cure me he told himself. He did not ease himself into the water. It might be said that he plopped in. He screamed when the first shock assailed him. Having barely survived it he shuddered and spluttered like a man demented as the cold touched every part of his body. Despairingly he started to sing. His voice trembled and shook. He could not sustain a single note no matter how hard he tried. There was one fearful moment when he felt totally paralysed. Panic-striken he erupted from the bath and landed on his behind on the slippery floor. Rising laboriously he dried himself thoroughly. After a few minutes he felt an improvement. His head still throbbed but the pain was now bearable. His hands were steady. He decided to risk a shave. Surprisingly he negotiated the business without a nick. He combed his hair and sat on the bed. He had no idea where he was. He was about to lift the phone when it occurred to him that he was naked. Hastily he pulled on his trousers. There was still some money in the fob; he was surprised at the amount. Probably cashed a cheque or two. All would be revealed in due course as the man said. He lifted the receiver and waited.

'Good afternoon, Mister Bowen.'

'Good afternoon. Where am I?'

A hearty girlish laugh from the other end.

'I'm serious. Where am I?'

'Poor Mister Bowen. I believe you.'

'Well?'

'The Neptune.'

'Galway?'

'Galway.'

'Thanks.' There was relief in his voice. Galway was less than three hours from home. He looked at his watch. Three forty-five. First he would eat something, pay his bill and then the road. He estimated that a leisurely speed should see him safely home with plenty of light in hand. He looked forward eagerly to the drive. At seven thirty as he drove through the outskirts of his home town there was still no sign of darkness. Like the skite which he had just put behind him he would never be able to present a detailed or coherent account of what happened next. He decided that it was too bright to go straight to the shop. Instead he headed for the Anglers' Rest. The place was deserted save for the proprietress Mrs Malone.

'You're back,' she said as though he had been away no longer than usual. There had in fact been mounting speculation all the week about his whereabouts. This had been replaced by genuine concern. In fact his cronies had decided to take the matter up with the Civic Guards should he fail to show up at the weekend. A skite was a skite but there were limits.

'Did you have a nice time?' Mrs Malone asked, hoping that the excitement did not show in her voice.

'Tip top,' Jimmy assured her. 'Let's have a glass of Jameson will you?'

While she dispensed the order Mrs Malone considered which of Jimmy's cronies and which of her own friends she would ring first. Collecting the note which

56

he had tendered she excused herself, ostensibly to look for change. She made several phone calls, at the same time keeping an eye on Jimmy from the back lounge where the phone was located. She conveyed each individual disclosure in a tone that was little above a whisper. Jimmy sat silently sipping his whiskey unaware of what was going on. It had not occured to him that his prolongued absence might have generated disquiet. All his thoughts were concentrated in an effort to determine the rate at which the daylight was fading outside.

'All too soon,' he told himself, 'it will be dark.' Suddenly he rose. He had reached a decision. It was time for his visit to the river. The whiskey had left him groggy but it had also brought a welcome warmth. In this happy state he departed the Anglers' Rest and sauntered, at leisure, to the river side. Twilight hung between the river and the sky. In all too short a time darkness would envelope the scene and the magical fleeting moments of transition would be no more. Already the shadows were expanded to their fullest. Any moment now the last pale threads of evening would vanish into the dark tapestry of night. Jimmy Bowen proceeded apace towards his favourite tree. The world stood still or so it seemed. The mottled water moved soundlessly on. Jimmy Bowen stopped, arrested in his tracks by what seemed to be a female form standing under the wide branches of the syca-more. His heart fluttered. His breathing quickened. He peered prayerfully through the half-light, advancing slowly. There was no mistaking the form. It was definitely that of a woman. A flimsy headscarf adorned her averted head. A white mackintosh covered her slender frame. This cannot be, Jimmy Bowen told himself and yet the creature is there, living and breathing as sure as darkness is descending. He harrumphed delicately lest he startle her. She turned suddenly and in a thrice she was in his arms. All at once Jimmy Bowen knew that something huge, something altogether monumental had been missing from his life until that moment. The embrace lasted an eternity or so Jimmy thought. In reality it ended after half a minute. He dared not look at her face. He risked a hasty glance and was pleased with what he saw in the darkness. Her features were somewhat angular but pleasantly defined. A solitary tear or what he took to be a tear glistened on her cheek under the weak moonlight. This was to be expected. They had both waited for too long a time. He was equally overcome even if there was no tear to prove it. Gently he took her by a hand that melted immediately into his. Slowly they returned along the way he had come. Mrs Malone looked up apprehensively when the door opened. She always did. A pub was a pub and you never knew when a troublemaker might put in án appearance. The relief showed on her face when Jimmy Bowen entered. This was wiped away altogether and replaced by genuine amazement when she beheld his companion.

'Sweet, Sacred Heart,' she addressed her customers, ''tis Mousy Miller and she without her specs.'

All within earshot turned to stare. A hush fell over the bar. Mrs Malone allowed her eyes to focus on Jimmy Bowen. There was a sort of glow to him. He still stood beside the doorway in a total trance, Miss Miller by his side. It was as though they were waiting for somebody to direct them. There was a word somewhere for the way Jimmy Bowen looked. Mrs Malone could not bring it to mind at once. Moonstruck, that was it, moonstruck.

After a while one of Jimmy's cronies arose and located seats for the pair.

'I declare but she looks downright attractive,' Mrs Malone confided to the customer nearest her. 'A bit too much make-up maybe but, still and for all, attractive. You'd hardly know her.' At the counter Jimmy dawdled happily for a moment or two.

'I'll have a Jameson,' he said.

'And Miss Miller?' Mrs Malone put the question.

'Miss Miller?'

'Behind you.'

Jimmy Bowen turned slowly and directed all his fading energies towards a hard look at his companion.

'Dammit if she isn't a dead ringer for Miss Miller.' He threw the observation over his shoulder to Mrs Malone.

'Ask her what she's having.' Mrs Malone's exasperation was beginning to show. Still Jimmy refused to budge. He just stood there with his back to the counter, happily if perplexedly contemplating his new-found love.

'What are you having, dear?' Mrs Malone called.

'Sweet sherry if you please,' came the demure and immediate reply.

'Dammit if she don't talk like her as well.' For the first time a note of alarm registered in Jimmy's voice. It conveyed itself immediately to Miss Miller. She looked about shamefacedly.

'Dammit,' Jimmy Bowen was saying as he looked at her from another angle, 'it is Miss Miller. Why didn't

59

'somebody tell me?' He looked foolishly from one watching face to another. An awesome silence had descended. Everybody looked everywhere, at Jimmy Bowen and Mrs Malone, at one another, at the ceiling, everywhere but at Miss Miller.

'Excuse me,' it was no more than a whisper but it was heard in every corner of the bar. It came from Miss Miller. She was on her feet.

'Your sherry.' Mrs Malone proferred the offering too late. Miss Miller was already on her way to the door which she closed gently behind her. There followed a short period of uneasy silence. Then came the clamour of relief. Everyone spoke at the same time. Jimmy Bowen alone was silent. He seemed dumbfounded. On his face was a look of utter perplexity. Still reeling he walked slowly towards the door. For an hour or more he walked aimlessly through the streets. Slowly, painfully, sobriety returned to him. Eventually he found himself at his own shop window. He fumbled for his keys while he took stock of his reflection. He looked none the worse for wear, eyes a little tell-tale maybe, face a little drawn, white hair a little tousled yet, all in all, presentable enough. He located the appropriate key but could not bring himself to insert it in the lock. He stood undecided, weighing the keys in his palm, considering his reflection. He closed his eyes firmly and opened them again. This time he looked beyond the reflection. Slowly in his mind a hazy background of trees and river water began to take shape. Out of the darkening landscape a pair of human forms, male and female, their features as yet indiscernible, emerged side by side from the shadows and stood under the sycamore. Jimmy Bowen held his breath as the female form gracefully inclined its head in his direction. The radiant smile on Miss Miller's face was for Jimmy Bowen and Jimmy Bowen alone. This was beyond dispute. Her heart showed clearly on her face. It sang for Jimmy Bowen.

'Why not?' he asked aloud. 'Why not?' he asked turning from the window and addressing himself to the street at large. 'Why not?' he asked of the stars overhead, 'why not, why not, why not?' he asked as he hastened to the widow's house where Miss Miller sat inside her window hoping for the impossible.

# 5.   'The Teapots Are Out'

'I was present,' Dinny Colman boasted, 'the day the first shot was fired.'

'It wasn't a shot was it?' my mother prompted, noticing my bewilderment.

'Of course it wasn't,' Dinny replied, 'but in all wars household or otherwise, someone has to start things off. The wrong word in the wrong place at the wrong time will do just as nicely or suppose people was taking their supper and if someone was to get fat meat which didn't like fat meat while others which didn't care whether they got fat or lean was presented with lean that would do it. I seen it happen. It may seem a small thing but in the eyes of the victim a great wrong has been done. A man's supper has been destroyed and in this God-forsaken countryside a man's supper is about the only diversion he has before drawing the clothes over his head for the night.'

He flicked the reins and called 'Giddap!' The bobbing rump twitched. The ears pricked. The paces stretched and quickened. The wind sang in our ears and we had to raise our voices to be heard. We were travelling on the flat. It wasn't till the pace slowed as we climbed the first of the forbidding hills on the road homeward that I found the composure to ponder Dinny's remarks.

The house we have just left was a thatched, one storey farmhouse like our own. Indeed it was like every other farmhouse in the countryside with the difference that on the one we had lately vacated the thatch was hoary and rotten retaining not a glimmer of the rich burnished yellow which it once boasted. The whitewashed walls were long since brown-stained by the stinking, blackened rainwater which oozed and seeped from the reeking thatch. The small, deep-set windows afforded little or no light to the interior. Add to this the fact that they had not been cleaned for years save where the imprint of a palm had smoothed a lookout from which occasional visitors might be vetted. The run-down farm had been let year after year to a neighbour while the byroad from the main road to the house was no longer distinguishable from the rushy fields through which it ran. Famished, underfed bullocks stood waiting for hay in a large bawling herd just inside the main gate. They looked as if they hadn't eaten for days. The general picture was one of casual decay.

'The teapots was out when we landed and out when we left.' Dinny was speaking to my mother. The farm was owned by Neddy Leary. With him in the kitchen during our visit had been his wife Dolly and his sister Bridgeen. Because they had been partaking of some afternoon tea we had surprised them. Each was seated at a different table, Neddy at the large, main table which stood in the centre of the kitchen, his wife and sister at either side of the turf fire which smouldered under a large, black iron kettle. Each had wet and drawn their separate pots of tea and withdrawn with them to their respective positions. Bread, milk, butter and sugar were communal and could be had from an appointed area at the end of the main table. The remaining space was restricted, the preserve of Neddy Leary. In truth the smaller tables were no more than glorified butter boxes which had been upturned and covered with patches of spare tarpaulin.

We had heard the sounds of discord quite plainly as we neared the house. All three were involved. It had reached hysterical proportions just as my mother knocked upon the door. Suddenly there wasn't a titter to be heard. A grimy face appeared at the window and shortly afterwards a voice called, 'Come in.' By this time, however, Dinny Colman, who was never a man to stand on ceremony, had the door open. The disarray was quite evident.

'God bless all here,' he used the benediction to camouflage his extreme curiosity. Hastily Dolly Leary and her sister-in-law Bridgeen departed the hearth clutching their teapots and other relevant accountrements. They disappeared soundlessly into an adjacent room.

'Come in, come in,' Neddy Leary cried as though there had never been a word of disagreement. Dinny Colman made immediately for the hearth and stood with his back to it so that the whole kitchen could be kept more easily under observation.

'Servant boys don't know their place no more,' Neddy Leary addressed himself to my mother at the same time rising and ushering us both to the hearth where he bade us sit on the chairs which had just been abandoned. This left Dinny with no choice but to move to one side. Using heavy black tongs Neddy Leary set himself the task of re-arranging the turf fire. This he managed to do with a surprising degree of skill. In seconds it was a tastefully-constructed pile of glowing embers, quite pleasant to behold and radiating welcome warmth. He delicately banked it with sods chosen from an ancient tea-chest which stood nearby.

He declined, however, to sweep the hearth and surrounds clean of ashes. He managed to give the impression that this was a chore beneath his dignity.

'As soon as that kettle boils,' he politely informed my
mother, 'we'll wet a mouthful of tea and discuss your
business.'

Having said this his face hardened and he called out
in a loud voice, 'Come down here this instant.' As he
once more turned to my mother the harshness left his
face. 'They'll be down now to set the table,' he told her.
Meanwhile Dinny Colman had moved nearer the door
where he made a thorough investigation of that makeshift portal. He seemed determined to record every
contrary detail. He moved next to the farthest corner
overhead which was a hen-coop covered by lattice wire.
Several pullets and hens of the Rhode Island Red
species sat contentedly staring into space as though
drugged or dazed. Reaching upward Dinny thrust a
finger through the lattice and tapped the nearest of the
hens on its beak. There followed a soft, fruity clucking.

'Let those hens be!' The order came from Neddy
Leary. He had been noting Dinny's progress with
mounting displeasure. Dinny moved on to where a
picture of the Sacred Heart was barely visible through a
cracked, dust-covered glass frame. He took a deep
breath and expelled it in the direction of the picture.
His every action was a deliberate manifestation of his
amusement.

Dolly Leary was the first to arrive from the room.
'You know my woman don't you?' Neddy said. 'Indeed
I do,' my mother answered. Nevertheless she shook
hands with Dolly who looked far tidier now than when
we first entered. After a few moments, enough to allow

Dolly establish herself, Bridgeen Leary presented herself. 'And my sister,' Neddy said. Again there was a handshake.

'Will ye take an egg with the tea?' Neddy enquired and he lifted a black cannister with the tongs. It was half-filled with murky water the surface of which was partly covered with ashes.

'No thanks,' the three of us answered hastily, too hastily. My mother made amends by stating that we had partaken of our dinners just before we set out. Dolly and Bridgeen began to clear the table. They were watched closely by Dinny who had returned to resume a less familiar form of communication with the Rhode Island Reds. Between them the women of the house managed to spirit away all the unsightly objects which had first greeted us. In no time at all a tablecloth covered the table. There were cups and saucers, side plates and a large dish which contained an outsize pancake and the quarter of a currant loaf.

'Dang that kettle,' Neddy Leary said but just as he spoke the faint curling steam from its spout was suddenly transformed into a solid jet. He took himself to the table where a whispered consultation took place between himself and the two women. The argument concerned itself with which of the three teapots should be used for the occasion. One word borrowed another and it seemed as if the parley might erupt into a major row. Suddenly there was silence. An agreement had been reached. Dolly Leary raced to the room she had just left and returned at once with a brown earthenware teapot which was obviously being pressed into service for the first time. It was quickly rinsed with a gurgling squirt from the boiling kettle. Neddy arranged a circle

of small coals of a uniform size a few inches from the
fire and on these the freshly-made tea in its brand new
teapot was allowed to draw. While we waited Dolly and
Bridgeen made the joint observation that I was like my
father but had my mother's eyes. Meanwhile in the
hen-coop there was uproar. Dinny, the party responsible, had quickly removed himself from the scene of
the crime and was once again inspecting the door.

'Take a seat at once sir,' Neddy spoke curtly and
indicated a chair at the bottom of the table. Suspecting
that a limit might have been reached Dinny sat at once.
One by one we joined him at the table. Neither of the
household women sat till the tea had been poured.
Neddy sliced the pancake and the currant loaf. A tell-
tale, off-white vein ran through each of the pancake
slices. The dough had not risen. In the case of the
currant loaf the fruit had sunk to the bottom. Despite
this we would be obliged to partake of at least one slice.
Thereafter it would be possible to decline all pressure
to eat more. Gingerly we opted for the currant loaf. It
was heavy going. No crumb fell to the table or the floor
such was its soggy consistency. We managed to get it
down, however, and so placed ourselves in a position to
refuse all other offers. The household, having satisfied
itself that our wants were fulfilled, ate heartily until
nothing remained in the dish.

'Now,' Neddy Leary announced as he wiped his
mouth with the back of his hand, 'tell us what it was
that brought ye.'

'Not much,' my mother answered, 'just to find out if
you could give us your brother Tom's address in New
York.'

'With a heart and a half but tell us who belonging to

you is for America?'

'This boy here,' my mother informed him.

'He's young isn't he?'

'Old enough at sixteen,' my mother responded.

Neddy Leary sighed. 'The best age,' he agreed. 'They don't settle so well when they shove on in the years. That was Tom's age when he left. Never looked back. Made out fine for himself.'

Neddy's younger brother Tom Leary figured as a sort of intercessory between prospective American employers and the droves of young Irish boys and girls who emigrated yearly from the district. It was a genuine labour of love on his behalf and indeed it would be unthinkable for any intending emigrant not to contact him before leaving home. His house served as a home from home during those heartbreaking first weeks. It gave the youngsters a chance to absorb the strange, complex environment until such time as they were able to make some slight evaluation of the new situation for themselves.

'I'll get it for you right away,' Neddy said. He rose and entered another room to the left of the kitchen. Nobody spoke during his absence. My mother cleared her throat and was about to say something but changed her mind. Dinny Colman eased himself self-consciously out of his chair and betook himself to the hearth where he first looked up the sooty chimney before standing with his behind to the fire, hands behind his back. He stood with a knowing smile on his face, his lips pursed, issuing a sly, soundless whistle. Neddy returned with a writing pad, a bottle of black ink and a small well-thumbed notebook. Behind his ear was a wooden-handled pen with a rusty nib. His wife and sister cleared the table feverishly while he stood imperiously waiting behind his chair. His eyes scanned the table for signs of any object which might impair the work which was about to begin. When he sat the two women stood in attendance directly behind him no more than a foot apart. Even Dinny Colman was impressed by the ritual. He was made to feel that he was in the presence of a scribe. An inner sense told him that it was not a moment for levity. Laboriously Neddy Leary laid out his writing materials on the table. When he was settled properly in his chair he uncorked the ink bottle, having first held it up to the light for careful inspection in case it harboured any foreign bodies. Satisfying himself in this respect he next inspected the rusty nib. Not finding it to his satisfaction he thrust it into his mouth, twirling it round and round several times therein and then proceeded to suck it as though it were a lollipop. Removing it he held it close to his eyes for final inspection. He dried it by the simple expedient of rubbing it against the sleeve of his coat. He then wet the thumb of his right hand with his tongue, lifted the notebook eye-high and thumbed through its tattered pages until a deep sigh of satisfaction intimated that he had found what he had been looking for.

'Thomas Ignatius Augustine Leary,' he chanted the words with due solemnity. 'Two forty-seven, East Two Sixty-second Street, City of New York, United States of America.' He concluded with an American twang. He then carefully proceeded to copy the address onto the notepaper. As he wrote not a pin could be heard to fall, a feather to alight, a heart to flutter, until he had almost completed his task. Quite out of the blue, you might say almost sacrilegiously, his sister Bridgeen covered part of her bosom with one hand and all of her mouth with the other before emitting a clearly audible gasp that shattered the concentration of the scribe as though a shotgun had been discharged over his head. His reaction was not to erupt from his chair mouthing blasphemous barrages in his sister's direction. He merely folded his hands while the colour of his face changed to a ghastly hue. A nerve-jangling silence of several moments ensued. Neddy Leary closed his eyes and spoke.

'Is there somebody present with something to say?' His voice shook with emotion. It was evident that he was making mighty efforts to control himself.

'It was me made the noise,' Bridgeen replied without a hint of apology in her voice.

'Why so?' Neddy was now drumming his fingers inquisitorially on the table.

'Because,' said his sister sarcastically, 'that's the old address.' So flaring a transgression was this that it simply had to be ignored. To contradict the head of the house in the presence of strangers could not be brooked no matter what. In the circumstances the only alternative was to pretend the woman had not spoken. Without haste Neddy finished off the address, rose, held it to the fire and allowed the ink thereon to dry. While he was thus engaged his wife committed the second cardinal error of the afternoon.

'If you're not careful you'll burn it,' she said. From the expression on his face it was plain that Neddy had decided to treat this comment with the same detachment as the other. When the ink had dried he folded the sheet of notepaper and handed it to my mother. His hands trembled and a furious fire burned in his dark eyes.

'I wish the boy luck,' he said gently, 'and now if you have no further business you might like to be shortening your road.'

'Of course,' my mother agreed, 'and let me thank you for your kindness.'

A sensitive woman she could readily presage the signs of the approaching storm. Any moment now the lightning would flash and the thunder roll and crack. The barely restrained winds of rage were already rustling dangerously. One could almost run one's fingers over the bristling tension.

'Time to go,' my mother ushered me to the door which Neddy Leary had obligingly opened for us. As ever Dinny Colman was inclined to dawdle. He posed affectedly in the doorway as though admiring the landscape while all he really wanted was to savour the beginnings of the oncoming conflict. He savoured it alright but not in the manner he would have liked. Behind him stood Neddy Leary waiting to close the door so that he might give rein to his anger. When Dinny refused to budge Neddy drew back his right foot and forcefully impressed the side of his boot on Dinny's buttocks making him to buck forward unceremoniously till he found himself on all fours. As soon as the kick was implanted Neddy banged the door shut the better to begin the domestic dissension in earnest. Outside after Dinny had recovered himself we marvelled at the indoor commotion. The first shot was fired in this instance when the ink bottle came flying through the window. Then came the clangour of human voices upraised and distorted till they seemed inhuman. It was a wanton, reckless, irascible strife. There was the sound of splintering wood mingled with the crash of breaking crockery. Add to this the noisesome jangle of cannisters, pannies, gallons, buckets and other tin missiles and some idea of the general bedlam will be conveyed.

The climax came with a mighty crash followed by the terrified clucking of badly-maimed hens. The hen-coop had fallen; whether by accident or design we could not determine. Suddenly there was silence. The battle was over. The door opened and a file of Rhode Islanders staggered and limped out from the scene of the fray. In the kitchen Neddy Leary sat at the table with his head in his hands. His wife and sister sat holding their sides at either side of the hearth. A lifeless hen lay sprawled on the floor. There was debris everywhere.

'Come along,' my mother said, 'they'll need to be alone now.'

'The teapots will be out forever after this,' Dinny Colman forecasted. He was still peeved at the way he had been treated by Neddy Leary. Reluctantly he followed us to the pony and trap. As we climbed the second hill Dinny was still muttering to himself over the injustice which had been done to him.

'Tell us about the very first shot,' I said. He mulled over the suggestion for a while.

'I worked there at the time,' he began. 'It was a fine place then carrying twenty milch cows and two score of dry stock. There was only the pair of them, Neddy and the sister. Tom had gone to the States to make his fortune. Neddy one night took it into his head to carry Dolly Mack home from a dance in the village. He made a habit of the thing after that and it was no time at all before the pair decided to marry. The trouble started the second day after the marriage. We were after coming in from the meadow. The new wife laid the table and put the eggs on to boil. Bridgeen sat near the fire darning a sock. Things was quiet and peaceful.

'"Will you eat one egg or two?" Dolly asked of Neddy.

'"Two if you please," said he.

'"Will you eat one egg or two?" she says to me.

'"Two if you please," said I.

'"Will you eat one egg or two?" she says to Bridgeen Leary, her sister-in-law.

'"Will I eat my own eggs is it?" she thrun back at Dolly. That was the first shot to be fired between the two and of course Neddy was soon drawn into it. The teapots came out soon after that and from the looks of things today they'll stay out for all time.'

# 6.   Guaranteed Pure

Willie Ramley came to Ireland for one purpose, to marry a virgin. In a New York tavern he had been informed by a man with a brogue as thick as a turnip that Ireland abounded in colleens of this calibre.

'How will I know she's a virgin?' Willie Ramley asked.

'You'll know,' the man with the brogue assured him.

'But how?' Willie Ramley persisted.

'Take my word for it,' the man with the brogue had said, 'when the time comes all will be revealed.' This had been the gist of the impartation.

Willie was halfway through his second month in Ireland and contrary to his expectations nothing whatever had been revealed. He had travelled far and wide but none of the girls he had encountered had appealed to him. The only one he had questioned regarding her virginity tagged him straight off with a right cross which would have done justice to a Golden Gloves middleweight. He ruefully pondered the advice tendered by the man with the brogue.

'All will be revealed,' he had said. It had been late on Saint Patrick's night. The man with the brogue whose name he had forgotten was regarded as something of a seer by the other patrons of the tavern. They treated him with deference and placed double whiskies in front of him from time to time for no apparent reason other than to bask in his favour. Willie could not remember how the conversation had started. All he recalled was that he had babbled out the story of his life concluding

74

with the latest and most tragic chapter which contained
the sordid details of how his latest girlfriend had been
two-timing him. The seer had placed a hand on his
shoulder and looked him straight between the eyes.
With the other hand he handed him an untouched glass
of whiskey.

'Drink that,' he had said, 'and take note of what I tell
you.'

Willie Ramley did as he was bade.

'You see before you,' said the seer, 'a man who was
once in the same quandary as yourself. My face is
wrinkled now and my hair is grey but I was a sparkling
fellow once eager for love and living. These same grey
hairs and wrinkles have been acquired at immense
expense. They, therefore, give me the right to advise a
young chap like yourself, not to pontificate mark you,
but to advise.' Wiping a tear from his eye he handed
Willie Ramley a second glass of whiskey.

'Wait,' Willie had said, 'let me buy you one.'

'No,' the seer had countered. 'All those who come
bearing me drinks have availed of my sagacity at one
time or another. Should you and I meet again and
should my counsel have proved to be beneficial I will
expect a whiskey or two by way of compensation but
for the present please to regard these drinks which you
see before me as much yours as mine.'

Willie nodded in agreement not wishing to interrupt
with facile thanks the verbal flow of this most gracious
old gentleman.

'When I was your age,' the sage continued, 'I jumped
into matrimony with the first good-looking girl I saw.
As a consequence the union was a disaster. It lasted
three weeks. I was married secondly within six months

and when that failed after a shorter period I vowed nevermore to marry. Oh vain resolve. In no time at all I was married again. You see my dear boy I was a martyr to matrimony. Seven times in all I ventured into the matrimonial stakes and seven times I came a cropper.'

At this juncture Willie Ramley felt constrained to put in a short spake.

'I would marry only once,' he said. The seer was about to utter a caustic comment but something in the young man's demeanour stayed him.

'I know how you feel,' he said, 'but marrying only once might not be so simple.'

'I realise that,' Willie told him, 'but I am determined to succeed.'

'Then,' said the sage placing his hand upon the young man's shoulder for the second time, 'you must be doubly careful.'

'Counsel me please,' Willie begged him. 'Counsel me I beseech you before the years catch up with me and I am left to languish alone.'

'This is what you must do,' the seer said with a solemnity which became the problem. 'You must betake yourself to Ireland from which sainted spot my mother, God rest here, emigrated to these less virtuous climes. She was truly an angel if ever there was one outside the sacred precincts of Heaven.' Here the sear paused to acknowledge receipt of a wholesome shot of whiskey from a grateful client.

'Because you are pure yourself,' the sage continued after he had sipped from the fresh bumper, 'you seek a creature of equal purity.'

Willie Ramley nodded eagerly. All his instincts firmly intimated that he had stumbled at last upon an authentic oracle.

'Do not,' said the sage, 'let yourself be carried away by the first pretty face nor by some coy damsel who will seem to be the answer to all your dreams. Be patient and the right girl will show herself. There will be something about her, something special that will set her apart from all others. This particular something will be as much in evidence as the nose on your very own face. It will be as clear as though it were stamped upon her back. Go now and keep you wits about you. Be continent in your ways and true to your ideal and she will make herself known to you in the manner in which I have indicated.'

So saying the sage lifted both hands in an elaborate flourish indicating that he had said all he was going to say. Willie Ramley departed the scene and for weeks was fully absorbed by all that he had been told. He finally resolved that there was nothing for it but to travel to Ireland and it was thus that he found himself after six weeks, as far from attaining to his aspiration as he had been when he first set foot on the green land of Erin. Now, with less than a fortnight's time remaining to him he began to grow anxious and despaired of ever achieving his goal. So we find him in this despondent mood seated on a turtog of snipegrass overlooking the vast beach of Ballybunion on a bright afternoon in the month of June.

Overhead seagulls mewed in the scented seaside air whilst around the human race disported itself as though fine days were at a premium. Elders paddled in the shallow shorewater whilst young men ventured beyond their depth endeavouring to test the concern of those inshore females for whom they had a special eye.

Toddlers toddled, back and forth to the tide. Small boys and girls breathlessly shaped castles of sand with shovel and bucket whilst a golden-skinned lifeguard lorded it over all who sported in his domain. In short it could be said that everybody was happy except Willie Ramley.

Tired of sitting in one place he decided to venture up-town with a view to imbibing a cool drink in one of the resort's many excellent hostelries. As he dandered along idly flicking empty cigarette and matchboxes with newly-purchased sandals he was almost run down by a bus. Had it not been for the fact that a passer-by hollered an alarm he might well have been injured. He managed to catch the bearest glimpse of his bene-factress, a shy young female who immediately averted her not unpretty head the moment she found his gaze turned in her direction. For a moment he stood un-resolved outside the door of a popular tavern. The words of the seer came drifting back to him. He decided to investigate further. The young lady was by now out of sight but it seemed to Willie that she was one of a party of females which had been on its way to the beach. He proceeded at a lively pace until he found the party once more within his ken. It consisted of five members. He followed at a discreet distance not wish-ing to overplay his hand and thus destroy his chances altogether. The party descended a stone stairway to where an array of ancient bathing boxes stood facing the shimmering sea. There followed some brief negoti-ations with the proprietor after which the five took possession of a similar number of the rust-wheeled wooden structures.

Willie Ramley carefully noted the box into which his

Lady Bountiful had disappeared. There was nothing for it but to wait until she came out. A strange sensation began to assail him, a composition of excitement and expectancy. He guessed that the five were countryfolk. He deduced this from the way in which they had looked around and about when they arrived at their destination. It was also apparent from their simple apparel and the way they carried themselves that they were daughters of the soil. He had expected a chaste emergence from the bathing boxes but he was totally unprepared for the sight which met his eyes. Each of the five was decked out in a long shift which fell to the toes and which concealed all the shapeliness thereunder. The shifts were off-white in colour and the material lightweight. What Willie Ramley could not know was that these full-length costumes were the common bathing attire of the people of the countryside. Thrifty souls that they were these frugal females rarely visited emporiums for the material which went into the making of their underclothes and beach attire. The flour which was used for the making of the daily bread came, as a rule, in calico bags of one hundred and twelve pounds or one hundredweight. When the flour was used up the bags were thoroughly washed and dried. The textile was used to make shifts, slips and knickers not to mention football togs and bedclothes. While the numerous town and city people on the beach might regard the calico-clad countrywomen with some amusement they, nevertheless, refrained from showing it. This could well be because they themselves had only recently emerged from country backgrounds.

Despite the lack of design the shifts sat well on their owners as they moved in stately formation from bathing boxes to shore with their heads held high to show how little they cared about what others thought. Their leader was a formidable, mightily-busted lady of late middle years, tall and broad-shouldered with aquiline features and a bearing which suggested that she was capable of defending herself and her charges in the unlikely event of an attack. The others were younger by far, late teens or early twenties so that Willie could not be blamed for concluding that the matriarch was more than likely the mother of the four. They walked demurely behind her looking neither left nor right. The girl who had prevented Willie's collison with the bus brought up the rear and it was clear that under the shapeless shift there was a body as beautiful as the imagination could conjure up. Reaching the water they proceeded along its edge to a spot where no other human soul was in evidence. Here, prompted by the matron, the young ladies entered the sea and after much skipping, leaping and shrieking accustomed themselves to its cold but salving wavelets. Then, dutifully while the matron kept a lookout in the background, the four faced themselves to the distant horizon and lifting the fronts of their shifts liberally sprinkled the exposed part of the anatomy with handfuls of cleansing sea water. The matron herself did not enter the water at all, content in her role of mother hen, repelling the curious with the most intimidatory of looks and doughty of stances. As soon as the girls had finished they chastely lowered their shifts and turned their backs to the very same horizon. The first exercise was repeated until the matron was satisfied that each was adequately bathed. Mustering her charges in a single file she resumed her position at the head of the column. Proudly and gracefully they returned the way they had come. Willie Ramley decided to make a closer inspection. He strode seawards with what he hoped was a casual air, pouting his lips into an indifferent whistle, giving the impression that he was an innocent holiday-maker lost in a private world of his own. Warily he circled round the matriarch as she led her brood to the boxes. His aim was to keep pace with the group from the rear so that he could better observe the lady of his choice. As he neared completion of his arc their eyes met ever so fleetingly but in that split-second exchange he lost his heart irrevocably. Again he recalled the seer's advice, 'Do not let yourself be carried away by a pretty face.'

There was more, however, to this young lady than a pretty face. Of that he was certain. He fell in behind and then he saw for the first time the word 'Sunrise' imprinted in faded red letters on the back of the shift. Willie Ramley would have had no way of knowing that this was the brand name of the popular variety of flour greatly favoured by the countryfolk of the time. The letters were in large capitals and underneath there was a longer inscription in faded black Italics.

Anxious to acquaint himself with its contents he closed the gap between them until the lettering was easily legible. 'One hundred and twelve pounds,' it said, 'guaranteed pure.'

He repeated the words over and over again to himself but it was only when the object of his interest had disappeared into her bathing box that the full significance of the latter part of the seer's advice impressed itself upon him. What was that he had said again, something about a special mark or sign that would set his

wife-to-be apart. But what were the precise words?
Slowly they came back to him.

'There will be something about her. . . It will be as
clear as though it were stamped upon her back.' Those
were the exact words as far as he could recall. No
further evidence of the girl's character was needed. He
waited impatiently for her re-emergence.

For the remainder of his holiday Willie Ramley
embarked upon a consistent and most earnest suit.
Morning, noon and night he waited upon her. The girl's
mother was impressed by his undeviating devotion and
when at length Willie had prevailed upon the young
lady to say yes the mother approved unreservedly and
the pair were married. The honeymoon, as was to be
expected, was spent in Ballybunion and on the first
night of what turned out to be a most blessed union the
blushing bride presented herself to her husband clad in
nothing but the long shift which carried on its back the
inscription: 'One hundred and twelve pounds. Guaranteed pure.' And indeed it must be said here that never
was a product so truthfully advertised.

# 7.   The Last Great Hare-Hunt
## of Ballycoolard

Han Boulter opened the American-stamped envelope
and extracted the letter. With great care she unfolded
the crisp, almost transparent notepaper to discover
three one hundred dollar bills taped to the opening
page. Normally the American letter might contain ten
or twenty dollars, even as much as fifty at Christmas
but this latest sum was exceptional although not unprecedented. It could only mean one thing. Her
brother, Monsignor Pat, pastor of Saint Sara's parish in
Louisville, Kentucky, would be coming home to his na-
tive Ballycoolard for an extended holiday in the not-
too-distant future. Before addressing herself to the
letter's contents Han Boulter rolled the notes into a
pencil-thick tube and deftly deposited them in the
depths of her ample bosom.

As expected the letter contained details of the monsignor's proposed itinerary. Alarm gathered on Han's
composed features as she calculated the nearness of her
brother's arrival. In less than a week he would be land-
ing at Shannon. There was much to be done. The house
would have to be painted inside and out, his room heat-
ed, his bed aired. The neighbours would have to be
told. He delighted in being received on his arrival by all
his old friends. Plentiful and varied stocks of drink
would have to be laid in. The monsignor imbibed all
kinds. In addition he was a gracious and magnanimous
host. Often he would sit until dawn with the friends of

his schooldays recalling colourful incidents from their salad days. Needless to mention these excursions into the past required to be fuelled by good quality spirits. It would be unthinkable for stocks to run out at the height of the reminiscing.

Then there was the question of meeting him at the airport. That would be the least of her worries, however. There would be no scarcity of volunteers for this highly-prized undertaking. The chore, more than likely, would be allotted by simple right of propinquity to her near neighbour Danny Doble. Danny had other privileged claims. He was distantly related to the Boulters and was it not he who was the monsignor's constant companion when they roved over the wild uplands of Ballycoolard in childhood days. Anyway wasn't it well known that Monsignor Pat was addicted to Danny's company above all others in the townland. As soon as Han Boulter had thoroughly absorbed every item of relevance in the letter she immediately launched herself into the drawing up of a comprehensive list of essentials to provide for her brother's stay. After one of these she erected a large question mark. The item in question was hare-soup. This one-time delicacy was reputed to be the ideal antidote for common or garden hangover. Indeed, as she recalled, Monsignor Pat was more partial to her own particular recipe than to any other broth or brew available locally. He literally lapped it up. The flesh of the hare was never eaten in the countryside. Traditionally this creature of the wild was associated with the fairy folk. Add to this the fact that the flesh was not particularly gustable or visually attractive and you were nearer the true reason.

Han was well aware that hares were scarce and had

been for a number of years. Some blamed modern fertilisers. Others who would not disagree with this altogether put it down to drainage as well. They maintained that the hare's natural and ancient sanctuaries were being transformed into viable grasslands where cover quickly disappeared after grazing or cutting. Still, Han Boulter felt, one solitary hare should not be too hard to come by. She resolved to refer this matter to Danny Doble. For him it would merely be a labour of love. If there was a hare within a radius of five miles Danny would discover its whereabouts and see that the animal was executed summarily for soup-making purposes.

When word spread that Monsignor Pat was coming on holiday there was much rejoicing all over Ballycoolard. After a winter which had truly tested the character of the hill people the first whispers of the amiable cleric's impending arrival added a special flavour to a newly arrived spring which was little milder than the recent winter. There would be trips to Killarney, to football and hurling matches regardless of distance. There would be hooleys to which all well-behaved people would need no invitation. The first person to whom Han divulged the sensational news was Danny Doble. She also conveyed her worries about the likelihood of a hare scarcity. He dismissed her fears.

The first thing he did having advised his cronies about the monsignor's visit was to arrange a meeting for that very night at the crossroads pub. Here, in front of a blazing turf fire, they discussed ways and means of capturing a hare.

'It would be a terrible thing,' Danny Doble told his listeners, 'to have no hare after he coming all of that

85

long journey for a drop of hare soup.' Murmurs of approval greeted this pronouncement.

'Time is of the essence,' Danny went on. 'A hare would need to be hanging three days before he's fit for the pot and we have only six days in all so hear is what I propose. We will appoint a man to reconnoitre Ballycoolard from top to bottom, from one end to the other. He will set out tomorrow morning and report back here to us tomorrow night. We will then prepare ourselves for the greatest hare hunt ever to be carried out in this part of the world. We will begin after first Mass on Sunday morning.'

Cries of 'hear-hear' and other expressions of approval were readily forthcoming. Only one question remained to be resolved. Who would be chosen for the task of inspecting the countryside? Names were mentioned but their proprietors were either too young or too old, too short-sighted or too near-sighted. In the end the name of Bronc Muldoon was mentioned most. He had earned his nick-name the hard way. A bare-back rider of asses, ponies and mules from the moment he could walk he had fallen off many times, nearly always upon his head. This had left him permanently confused, a sort of child of the wilds who was closer to nature than any living person in Ballycoolard. There was no questioning his stamina or speed. Out of the way places in hill and dale were his favourite haunts. He was young and he was eager. Most important he was fitted for little else.

The instructions given him were that he was to scour the region until he sighted a hare or any number of hares. Under no circumstances was he to disturb or molest the creatures. Most hares lope indolently around a chosen area or rest in their secluded forms unless agitated by hounds or fowlers. For the most part they tend to ignore disinterested humans so that the Bronc's intrusion into hare country was not likely to provoke any dramatic departure from one area to another.

'Make your sighting and proceed about your business until you have the whole of Ballycoolard covered,' was the advice tendered by Danny Doble. The elders in the company recalled likely hare habitats while the Bronc assiduously repeated all he was told in a loud voice. A rough map of the district was drawn up by the schoolmaster. On it a starting place was prominently marked and from this point a heavy red line ran circuitously through the prescribed terrain until the ultimate boundary was reached. Then and not till then was the Bronc to return home. It was expected that he would encounter more than one hare and more than one group of hares provided his search was industrious and comprehensive.

'In the event of this happening,' Danny Doble warned, 'you will make immediate recourse to your map and mark your sightings conspicuously.'

'Yes,' the schoolmaster put in, 'and in so doing you will provide us with the blueprint of our hunt and spare us much time and labour on Sunday.'

The group stayed on in the pub after closing time recalling to mind memorable hunts and doughty hares which once extended them beyond the limits of their endurance. The following morning the Bronc Muldoon was up at first light. His widowed mother, aware of the importance of the task ahead of him, provided him with a breakfast fit for a ploughman. The Bronc as was his wont left not a single morsel on the plate. While he was eating she packed a substantial lunch. This together with a quart bottle of milk she placed in an ancient haversack which had seen better days. Her last act was to douse him liberally with holy water.

The first thing the Bronc did after he left the house was to eat the lunch his mother had prepared for him. He then sought and discovered a shady, dry shelter where he slept for a few hours. When he awoke his conscience got the better of him. Without further ado he made a hasty study of the map and proceeded to the starting point. Darkness had fallen by the time he reached the pub at the crossroads. A large crowd had foregathered. Around the open hearth fire were seated the elders and men of stature such as the schoolmaster and Danny Doble. Breathlessly the Bronc recounted all he seen. He made no mention whatsoever of hares until pressed by his listeners to do so.

'I never in all my born days,' said the Bronc, 'seen so many hares in the same place at the same time.'

'Where exactly was this?' Danny Double asked.

'At the end of Jackeen Quinlan's cutaway,' the Bronc promptly replied. At the same time he produced the map where he had marked the exact spot as instructed.

'You say you never saw so many hares?' Danny Doble sought confirmation of the Bronc's announcement.

'Never saw so many,' the Bronc told him, 'but for I watching my step,' he continued, 'I would have been standing down on the devils.' For the remainder of the night he was handsomely plied with porter. Towards closing time he was inclined to ramble but no one was perturbed by this. The map was in the safe keeping of the schoolmaster and that was all that mattered. Plans were carefully laid for Sunday's hunt. It was decided that the force would split up into two parties and arrive at the location from two opposite approaches. This would reduce the chances of the hares escaping.

At early Mass on Sunday Father Morrigan, the parish priest, gave his blessing to the hunt and immediately afterwards Danny Doble reviewed the entire party in front of the church. It consisted of thirty-seven men and boys, three good-class coursing grey-hounds and two score other dogs of every conceivable breed and size. Rain fell heavily from the outset obscuring surrounding fields and bogland but failing to dampen the spirits of the hunters. At the crossroads pub the party divided itself in two. The schoolmaster was the unanimous choice to lead one half while none contested Danny Doble's right to command the other. Ahead went the dogs and beaters while the rest followed in high spirits. Quickly the miles fell behind but no hare was encountered. This was to be expected. In his reconnaissance of the day before the Bronc Muldoon had discovered no hare until he reached Jack-een Quinlan's cutaway. It was now more apparent than ever that they were on the right track. All the time the rain fell mercilessly but not a whisper of complaint was to be heard from human or hound. Some of the party who had not anticipated the continuing downpour were drenched to the skin. If anything this made them more resolute. Rivulets of rainwater ran downward from foreheads to chins from whence they seeped under shirt collars and scarves. The dogs were silent now. They still panted hopefully, ears ever ready to prick at the sight of game, egged on by their handlers whenever they snapped at each other or dawdled to sniff at imaginary spoors. The handlers were otherwise silent as were the rest of the hunters. Above the laboured breathing of the older members of the band was to be heard the juicy squelching of rain-sodden footwear. Still they proceeded at a sapping pace until shortly before noon the Doble contingent found itself confronted by the vast expanse of Jackeen Quinlan's cutaway. There was, as yet, no indication that the second party had arrived. They waited silently for the pre-arranged signal. This was to consist of two blasts, one long and one short on a referee's whistle. Danny Doble's keen eyes swept the cutaway for signs of life. He expected none for the cover was intense but there was always the outside possibility that a young hare would be panicked into breaking at the unexpected blasts of the whistle. The cutaway covered an expanse of fifty or so acres. It abounded in heavy snipe grass, sally groves and fraochan bushes. The general colour was a brown-stained yellow, an ideal background for wildlife. There was no doubt in Danny's mind but that it contained hares. It would be hard to imagine a likelier haunt for these timid denizens of the wilds.

Suddenly came the shrill whistle blasts from the other end of the cutaway. A hen pheasant lifted herself from a hidden nest and flapped noisily out of view.

'Right men.' The command came from Danny Doble. Dogs whined and squealed and took off in all directions. The hunting party howled and hollered and lay with their heavy sticks into the snipe grass. Yard by yard they worked themselves towards their approaching comrades.

'Any second now,' Danny Doble called out, 'any second now they'll break. Be ready.' The dogs sensing the orgy of slaughter set up a deafening outcry. Eventually both parties met in the centre of the cutaway. Most were fit to collapse after the daunting foray through the snipe grass.

'Where are all the hares?'

The words were spoken by the youngest member of the gathering. Nobody was prepared to answer his question. The older members looked about them in disbelief and then at each other in perplexity. The same outspoken question was written on every rain-washed face.

'Where are the hares?' Angry mutterings followed. Then came the most pertinent question of all. 'Where was the Bronc Muldoon?' As the party consulted with the Bronc's neighbours it transpired that he had not taken part in the hunt. He had, in fact, not been seen at all that morning. Nobody had called for him. All had presumed that because he was an integral part of the hunt he would automatically be present. The party returned to their respective homes in a despondent state. They had failed miserably in their task. All they had to show for the day's outing were soggy clothes down to the very undergarments and running noses which were surely the harbingers of heavy colds and aching joints. There was not a man or boy in Ballycoolard who didn't heartily curse the Bronc Muldoon that night.

Inevitably the blame for the entire debacle having flitted from one eminent member of the hunt to another attached itself to Danny Doble. It was he after all who organised the expedition into Jackeen Quinlan's cutaway. Nobody said so to his face but he sensed the disillusionment when he visited the crossroads pub the night after the hunt. There was no outright hostility nor was there the slightest dispraise for the way he had handled things. He was wise enough to keep his mouth firmly shut regarding the events of the day before, lest he provoke spoken disapproval. Oddly enough nobody blamed the Bronc.

'Not the full shilling,' was the worst that was said about him. Danny, however, was adamant that the blame should find its proper resting place. Shortly before closing time the Bronc put in his customary appearance.

'What'll you have?' Danny Doble asked. The Bronc, although suspicious of the offer, intimated that he would not be opposed to a pint of stout. Danny permitted him a first swallow before standing him with his back to the open fire in full view of everybody.

'Tell us now,' said Danny in a pleasant voice, 'exactly how many hares you saw in Jackeen Quinlan's cutaway?'

A hush fell on the company. The Bronc made no attempt to answer. Danny repeated the question this time in a more demanding tone. The Bronc swallowed hard and moistened his lips. He looked from face to face but nowhere was there sympathy to be found. Neither was there condemnation.

'Twelve hares was what I saw all told,' he blurted out.

'How many?' Danny asked in his most challenging tone.

'Six,' from the Bronc.

'How many?' Danny had him on the run and knew it. He pressed home his advantage. 'Come on Bronc. How many?'

'Three.' The Bronc bent his head rather than look his accuser in the eye.

'For the last time Bronc,' Danny was adamant now, 'how many hares did you see?'

Bronc made no verbal reply. He lifted the index finger of his left hand to indicate that one hare was all he had seen. The gesture failed to satisfy Danny Doble.

'Are you prepared to swear on your solemn oath that it was a hare you saw?'

Hangdog now the Bronc made no attempt to answer. He looked for an avenue of escape but there was none.

'What exactly did you see in Jackeen Quinlan's cutaway?' Danny asked after a while. The Bronc muttered an inaudible response.

'Louder,' came the relentless prompting of his interrogator.

'What I saw,' the Bronc blurted out the words, 'was Jackeen Quinlan's cat and not a hare.'

'Not a hare? And not three nor six nor twelve hares?' Danny persisted with the inquisition.

'Not three nor six nor twelve hares,' the Bronc replied.

'Only Jackeen Quinlan's cat?' Danny rose unsteadily as he launched the final poser. With the aplomb of a truly accomplished advocate he waited for the Bronc's confirmation.

'Only Jackeen Quinlan's cat,' the Bronc whispered. Danny Doble bowed to left and right as if to judge and jury, finished his whiskey and sauntered with his hands entwined behind his back into the starry world outside.

# 8.  Faith

The brothers Fly-Low lived in an ancient farmhouse astride a bare hillock which dominated their rushy fields. Tom Fly-Low was the oldest of the three. Next in age came Billy and lastly there was Jack.

Fly-Low, of course, was a soubriquet. The surname proper was Counihan. It was never used except by the parish priest once every five years when he read the Station lists.

In the year 1940 an Irish reconnaissance plane flew over the Fly-Low farm. At the time the brothers were in the meadow turning hay. As soon as the plane appeared they stopped work and lifting their hayforks aloft welcomed the unique intrusion. Acknowledging the salute the pilot dipped his wings.

'Fly low,' Jack Counihan called.

'Fly low,' shouted his brothers. 'Fly low, fly low,' they all called together. Alas the pilot was unable to hear them. In a few moments the plane had disappeared from view never again to be seen by the brothers Fly-Low. In neighbouring fields other haymakers heard the din. It was only a matter of time before the Counihans would become known as the Fly-Lows. It was no more than the custom of the countryside. It made for easy identification there being several other Counihan families in the nearby townlands.

Years later at the end of the Second World War there came one of the worst winters in living memory. When it wasn't awash with drenching rain the winds blew searingly and searchingly. There were times when it froze and times when it thawed, times too when it snowed till the hills turned white. In between there was sleet, that awful conglomeration which can never make up its mind whether it's rain, snow or good round hailstone. There had been ominous signs from October onwards. Gigantic geese barbs imprinted the skies from an early stage. The bigger the geese-barbs the blacker the outlook or so the old people said. On blackthorn and white were superabundances of sloe and haw, sure auguries these of stormy days ahead. All the time the moon, full and otherwise, was never without a shroud. Then came an awesome night in the middle of January. Before darkness fell cautionary ramparts of puce-coloured, impenetrable cloud were seen to make dusty inroads into an ever-changing sky. The wind blew loudly and as night wore on it blew louder still.

At midnight a storm of unprecedented savagery ravaged the countryside. Wynds of hay were carried aloft and deposited in alien fields miles away. Trees were flattened and suspect haysheds gutted but of all the destructive acts perpetrated that night none was so capricious as that which swept the slates from the roof of Tom Fly Low's bedroom. The rest of the house was left untouched. At half past one in the morning the oldest of the Fly-Low brothers found himself staring upwards into a swirling sky.

Wise man that he was he decided to stay abed till the storm spent itself. This it did as dawn broke mercifully over a devastated landscape.

After breakfast the brothers inspected the damage. Structurally there was nothing the matter. They came to the conclusion that a sufficiency of second-hand slates was all that was required to repair the roof. They knelt beside the kitchen fire and offered a Rosary in thanksgiving. Immediately afterwards the youngest brother Jack was commissioned to undertake the journey to the distant town of Listowel there to forage among the premises of builders' providers for the necessary materials. Tom Fly-Low who acted as treasurer to the household counted fifty pounds in single notes into Jack's hands while Billy went in search of the black mare. She would be tackled to the brothers' only transport, a large common cart with iron-banded wheels.

Jack shaved in the kitchen and changed into his Sunday clothes. He dipped a brace of calloused fingers in the holy water font which hung just inside the front door, made the Sign of the Cross and went out of doors to begin the eleven mile journey to the town. He was met in the cobbled yard by a fuming Billy. The mare had broken from the stable during the storm and was nowhere to be found. There was nothing for it but to walk to town and hope for a lift.

After the second mile Jack stopped and lighted his pipe. He sat in the lee of a densely-ivied hedge and allowed himself a brief rest. Around him the light green of well-grazed fields mottled with dung-induced clumps of richer grass shone in the winter sunlight. Birds sang in roadside bushes. Wearily he got to his feet and continued on his journey. As he did an ancient Bedford truck appeared around a bend at his rear. Before he had time to hail it the driver had changed gears and brought it to a halt. Thankfully Jack Fly-Low climbed into the cab.

The driver was a thin-faced, refined-looking man wearing a tattered black tam and faded overalls. After

Jack had thanked him there was silence for a mile or so.

'Don't I know you?' the driver asked.

'I don't see how you could,' Jack told him. 'I don't know you.'

'My name is Florrie Feery,' the driver introduced himself.

'And my name is Jack Counihan,' Jack responded.

Half an hour passed without another word. At last they found themselves in the suburbs of Listowel.

'Where here do you want to be dropped off?' Florrie asked. Jack Fly-Low mentioned the name of a prominent builders' provider, 'but,' said he, 'first I must stand you a drink.'

The first drink borrowed a second and a third at which stage they had taken possession of two seats near a small table in a cosy corner of the bar. A turf fire burned brightly in a fireplace nearby. When Florrie rose to order a fourth drink Jack protested. His business was pressing he explained. There was no time to spare.

'What can be so pressing?' Florrie asked, 'that won't keep till we've had a *deoch an dorais*?'

Instantly Jack felt ashamed. Here was this exceptional fellow who had picked him off the road when he might have been no more than a tramp or a common highwayman, who had asked for no reference when he opened the door of his cab, who only wanted to buy his round like any decent man. Over the fourth drink the conversation turned inwards on their personal business and respective families. Confidences were exchanged as a result of which Jack Fly-Low decided to divulge his reason for being in town. Florrie listened sympathetically and attentively.

'That's a coincidence,' he said half to himself, half to Jack, as soon as the latter had finished telling him about the disappearance of the slates.

'What is?' Jack asked.

'This chap near me back at home.'

'What about him?'

'Nothing. . . except that he has an old house destined for demolition.'

'And?'

'And,' Florrie paused to sip his whiskey, 'on the top of his house is the finest roof of second-hand slates you or me is ever like to see.'

'It was God made our paths cross this morning,' Jack Fly-Low said solemnly. 'Do you think your man might be induced to sell the slates off this roof?'

Florrie permitted himself a deep chuckle. 'Only this morning he asked me if I would be on the look-out for a buyer.'

Thereafter they spoke in whispers at Florrie's insistence. There was the danger, he pointed out, that every Tom, Dick and Harry would get wind of the slates before he had time to close the deal on Jack's behalf. Caution, therefore, was of the essence. Because of his regard for Jack he would lay strong claim to a family relationship which existed between himself and the gentleman who owned the derelict house. He was of the opinion he could purchase and deliver the slates for a mere thirty pounds. Like a flash Jack Fly-Low's right hand went for his inside pocket. Florrie laid a restraining hand on his shoulder.

'Not here,' he said, 'let's go in the back.'

In the makeshift toilet at the rear of the premises the thirty pounds changed hands. A gentleman to the last

Florrie insisted in handing back a pound in luck money. There were more drinks before the truck driver recalled that he had promised to purchase a load of turf in a distant townland. There was an emotional goodbye and a promise that the slates would be delivered not later than noon of the following Saturday.

It was close to midnight when Jack Fly-Low arrived home. Billy and Tom were waiting by the hearth for an account of the day's activities. They listened spellbound as the youngest brother recounted the details of the day's outing. They were particularly impressed with his account of Florrie. Jack regaled them with different facets of the man's character until well into the morning. Whenever he flagged he would be prodded or prompted by Tom or Billy. They longed for Saturday so that they might see this paragon for themselves.

Early on Saturday a tradesman arrived to ready the roof for the slating. By noon he was in a position to start work in earnest but as the day wore on there was no sign of Florrie.

'He'll come,' Jack assured the others, 'just give him time.'

Every hour or so a mechanically propelled vehicle could be heard passing on the public road which passed by the extreme boundaries of the farm.

'Hush,' Jack would call, 'that's him now. That's him surely.' The faces of the three brothers would light up expectantly whenever the noise of an engine was borne upward by the breeze. The tradesman smiled slyly to himself. There was the making of a good story here he told himself, a tale that would bear telling in the pub that night. At five o'clock he departed. He promised to return the moment the slates arrived.

The days passed but there was no sign of Florrie. Weeks went by, then months. Daffodils arrived to brighten the spring fields. The thorn buds quickened in the hedgerows but of Florrie and the slates there was no sign.

From time to time the tradesman would call to enquire if the materials had arrived. He volunteered to cover the roof temporarily with corrugated iron but the brothers would not hear of this. What would Florrie think? They had convinced themselves that he had been taken ill or that he had been involved in a serious accident.

The brothers Fly-Low had implicit trust in Florrie. Had not Jack spent a day with him, vetted him from all angles so to speak and convinced himself that he was an uncommonly fine fellow. Summer came and went and Tom's room still lay exposed to the elements. He moved to a settle bed in the kitchen. The brothers were agreed that it would be a breach of faith if they made any attempt to cover the roof before Florrie arrived. Arrive he would. Of that they were certain.

Whenever neighbours called to pass the time of day one or other of the Fly-Low's would interrupt the conversation if the noise of traffic came from the roadway.

'Hush, hush,' they would caution, 'that could be Florrie with the slates.'

It never was. In the houses around the neighbouring countryside the whole business of the slates became something of a standing joke. Whenever a vehicle was heard passing some member of the household was sure to say: 'Hush, hush now. That's Florrie with the slates.'

For years it was a catchcry with younger folk ever on the alert for any form of diversion. It was without malice. No one would intentionally make fun of the Fly-Lows. They were good neighbours, deeply religious and charitable to a fault.

As the years rolled on mention of Florrie became rarer and rarer in the Fly-Low kitchen. At night when the boozing of a lorry was heard in the chimney the brothers would exchange hopeful looks but no word would pass between them. Of the three Jack felt the disappointment most keenly. The others had not known Florrie like he had. Occasionally they might be forced to suppress nagging doubts and suspicions but having known the man in question he was never so affected.

The way Jack saw it any number of things could have happened. He recalled that Florrie was liberal with his money. This would not have escaped the notice of the numerous bar denizens who prey upon decenter types. Perhaps by now his body lay decomposed in some bog-hole or dyke. It was more likely, however, that an accident was responsible for his non-appearance. He had taken more than his fair share of drink on that memorable occasion in Listowel. For all Jack Fly-Low knew the poor fellow could be dead and buried long since or maybe it was how he lost his memory. He had heard of cases where the memory failed altogether after excessive consumption of doubtful whiskey.

Anything was possible. Inevitably Tom and Billy decided the roof should be covered. Otherwise the entire house would suffer. As a concession slates were not used. Instead sheets of corrugated iron were hammered into place by the tradesman. The new roof was laid on in the spring. In the winter of that year Tom Fly-Low passed away having succumbed to a bout of

pneumonia. His brothers were convinced that he corru-
gated-iron roof was responsible. They gave the room a
wide berth after Tom's burial.

Then one windy night in the spring of the following
year the distinct boozing of an oncoming lorry was
heard in the chimney. From the increasing volume of
the sound it was clear that it was heading for the house
of the Fly-Lows. Jack and Billy rose together, their
faces taut, not daring to breathe. His heart pounding
Jack opened the front door. Outside was a lorry. A
man was alighting from the cab. He was approaching
the doorway.

'Is it Florrie?' the barely whispered question came
from Billy who stood at his brother's shoulder. The
driver came nearer. Jack Fly-Low stood unmoving.
Beside him Billy trembled uncontrollably. The driver
was speaking:

'Is this Dinnegan's?'

'No,' Jack answered. 'Go back the way you came.
Dinnegan's is the next turn on the right.'

The driver was squat, coarse and throaty. Florrie had
been slender and tall, elegant almost. The driver re-
entered his cab, reversed and drove off.

In the kitchen Billy Fly-Low slumped against the
table. The excitement had been too much for him.
Unable to support himself he fell to the floor. A
strange, unearthly sound came from his throat. Jack
knelt and whispered an act of contrition into his
brother's ear.

Some months after the funeral a group of neighbours
came to visit Jack Fly-Low. During the interval
between the visit and the burial of Billy he had grown
gaunt and feeble. The neighbours were concerned. It

might be best if he sold the farm and moved to town where help would be at hand should any sudden misfortune befall him. No. He would never leave the old homestead. A housekeeper then? No. Why not let the farm? No. Jack Fly-Low was adamant. He would look after himself to the end. In spite of this the neighbours made an agreement between themselves that they would call regularly to see him.

The following December there came an unexpectedly heavy snow storm. A number of outlying houses were cut off for several days. Among these was the Fly-Low abode. As soon as the byroads were passable a neighbour made his way to the hillock. He found Jack in a sorry state. His breathing came irregularly and weakly. Often for long spells he would gasp for breath. The neighbour left hurriedly and found somebody to notify the priest and doctor. Quickly he returned and sat on the bedside holding Jack Fly-Low's hand while the numbered breaths grew fainter. The neighbour was relieved when at last he heard the sound of the priest's car in the driveway. Vainly Jack Fly-Low endeavoured to raise himself to a sitting position. His throat crackled but no words came. His lips moved but no sound issued forth.

'What is it Jack? What's the matter?' the neighbour asked anxiously. Gathering the last vestiges of his vanishing strength Jack Fly-Low opened his mouth.

'Florrie,' he whispered triumphantly before falling back on his pillow. His body slackened, the lips sealed themselves again but now there was the semblance of a smile on the shrunken dead face.

# 9.  Fred Rimble

Fred Rimble was born in Maggie Conlon's kitchen in Dirreenroe at three minutes past seven on the evening of 7 September 1979. The event was not marked by any unusual celestial manifestations nor was there the least furore in the more immediate circumjacence of Dirreenroe.

'Indeed,' said Maggie Conlon's son Jim at a later date, 'I would not have brought the poor creature into the world at all but for being driven to it by my mother's ear-ache.'

At seventy-five Maggie Conlon belied her age by several years. Her hair still retained most of its natural black. Her eyes were bright and clear. Her step was free of infirmity and while she would never admit to it the hearty appetite which she had enjoyed all her life still remained with her, completely unimpaired.

She should, therefore, have been fairly well pleased with the general state of her health and, of course, if you were also to take into account the fact that she was relatively well-to-do you should not be blamed for believing that her all-round lot was a happy one.

Alas the opposite was the case. Maggie Conlon was a hypochondriac. Local doctors could find nothing the matter with her, but hope springs eternal so Maggie fared as far afield as her means would allow and consulted unsuccessfully with several noted specialists. She then resorted to quacks after the fashion of all true hypochondriacs and despite temporary cures of the most dramatic nature continued to provide local

104

doctors and pharmacists with a solid source of income.

The mystery was that she managed to survive the vast and varied intake of potions and pills not to mention the liniments and lotions with which she harrassed the countless aches and skin diseases to which her hypersensitive exterior seemed always to be prey. The most malignant aspect of this particular type of hypochondria was while it failed to hasten the demise of Maggie Conlon it had dispatched her two husbands to early graves.

Both had been hard-working men who needed rest and care after their day's labours. Neither, unfortunately, was forthcoming from Maggie. From dawn till dark both husbands were on call. Poultices were constantly in demand as were hot drinks, gargles and numerous other medicaments. These necessitated regular journeys upstairs and downstairs all through the night. Fine if Maggie was available in the morning to cook a sustaining breakfast and provide a nourishing lunch pack or if she was on her feet in the evening with a warm welcome and a warmer meal. Instead she was confined to bed and during those rare intervals when no pain troubled her she went around with her head and face muffled, with her body totally covered and smelling all the time of powerful prophylactics.

Whether or not she succeeded in warding off occupational diseases and wayward draughts was anybody's guess but one thing was certain. The germs of romance which might have blossomed in perfumed surrounds into rich and rewarding love were slowly but surely exterminated by the deadly disinfectants in which her garments abounded. The marriages had started out well enough. In the beginning there had been affection, a close relationship in both cases which might have been nurtured into something more rewarding if Maggie had shown the least desire to relinquish her unnatural preoccupation with her health.

Jim Conlon was the sole outcome of both marriages presenting himself to the world shortly after the demise of his father, Maggie's second husband. At the time an unkind neighbour was heard to say that the poor man had precipitated his own death with the awful prospect that the issue might be female and that he would be faced with two Maggies instead of one. The truth was he died of fatigue. Maggie Conlon had worn him out just as she had worn out his predecessor. There are some men who thrive off selfish wives, who excel themselves as husbands in the face of such adversity. There are others who suffer in silence, waiting for death to rescue them. Maggie's pair were of this latter mould.

Her son Jim was a mild-mannered, easy-going fellow who asked little of the world. His job, a book-keeper in the local creamery, was undemanding. His wages were more than adequate. He lived with his mother. He might have married but progress in that direction was brought to an immediate halt as soon as any likely contender encountered Maggie.

One particular girl with whom he had made considerable headway spelt out her terms unequivocally after a visit to Maggie.

'I'm willing to marry you,' she told Jim, 'and I'm willing to devote the rest of my life to you but it will have to be in a town or city a long way from here.'

'I just can't walk out on her altogether,' he pleaded. 'After all she is my mother.'

'I'm not asking you to walk out on her,' the girl

explained. 'You can visit her from time to time and she can visit us if she feels like it. You have your own life to live and I'm sure your mother will accept this when you explain it to her.'

'I never heard the like,' Maggie Conlon had retorted bitterly when Jim had laid his cards on the table. 'I mean it's not as if I were asking the pair of you to come and live with me under this roof and anyway where are you going to get another job if you leave Dirreenroe? Have you thought of that?'

'Oh I'll get another job alright,' Jim assured her. 'With my experience that should be no trouble.'

The following afternoon Maggie Conlon lay in a hospital bed as a result of an inexplicable collapse on her way from the butcher's earlier that morning. The doctors were mystified. Her heart was strong, her pulse steady, her blood pressure normal. She was released after a week with a clean bill of health after Jim had declared that he would never leave Dirreenroe.

Now at thirty-one he began, at last, to see the writing on the wall. The constant complaining had begun to take its toll. At work he wondered what new malaise would be awaiting him when he arrived home. It was not till he found himself on the threshold of mental disintegration that he brought Fred Rimble into the world. That morning before he left for work his mother had complained of a severe backache. Jim had called the family doctor but that worthy could find nothing wrong. When Jim arrived home for lunch his mother was still in bed. The ache in the back had removed itself and was now resident in the neck. When he finally finished work he was surprised to hear it had ended up in the left ear after a horrendous journey from its

107

original starting place.

'I won't get a wink of sleep tonight,' she complained when he suggested she abandon the bed and share the stew which he had prepared for both of them. He pleaded in vain.

'I couldn't look at a bite,' she said which meant that she had eaten while he was at work. After he had washed and stowed the ware he returned to the bedroom. Her martyred face was barely visible through an opening in the red flannellette with which she had bound her head. The bed clothes were drawn tightly under her chin. Every so often a distraught moan punctuated her affected wheezing.

'No one has an ear like mine,' she whined.

'I don't know,' Jim spoke casually. 'A chap had his ear chopped off at the creamery today, his left ear.' Maggie Conlon raised herself painfully on her elbows.

'Had his left ear chopped off?'

'His left ear,' Jim confirmed.

'Was he from Dirreenroe?' Maggie removed the red flannellette the better to catch the answer.

'From Dublin,' Jim replied.

'Oh the poor man.' Maggie was all concern. 'What hospital did they take him to?'

'No hospital,' Jim told her.

'But I don't understand. You say he had his ear chopped off.'

'Yes. He had his ear chopped off.'

'And he didn't go to hospital?'

'As far as I know.'

Maggie sat upright in the bed. 'I'm afraid I don't understand.'

Jim rose from the side of the bed where he had seated himself. He sighed and went to the window. His gaze swept the evening sky before he spoke.

'He was demonstrating an electric potato peeler,' he explained slowly, 'and the next thing you know the damn thing stopped. He bent down right where the potato goes in and off she starts without warning.'

'And the ear?'

'He put it in a bucket of ice and clapped a handkerchief over the wound and then hit for Dublin to have it sewn back on.'

'What did you say his name was?' Maggie Conlon asked.

'Fred Rimble,' Jim replied.

'I don't know any Rimbles,' Maggie said.

'How could you when he doesn't come from around here. I told you he came from Dublin.'

When he arrived home for lunch the following day he found his mother up and about. The pain in the ear had partially disappeared and for a change a hot meal awaited him.

'Any news of Fred Rimble?' Maggie asked.

Jim was taken unawares but he took advantage of a mouthful of mashed potatoes to hide his surprise. As he masticated needlessly his imagination worked overtime. Finally he spoke.

'He's lucky to be alive is Fred Rimble.'

'Did he get back to Dublin?'

'Not off his own bat. He fainted in the car from loss of blood and crashed into a telephone pole.'

'Oh my God!' Maggie Conlon cried. 'What happened then?'

'He was taken by ambulance to Dublin. Apparently the ice spilled from the bucket with the impact of the

109

crash. The ear was thrown onto the roadway and could not be found. They fear a magpie may have made off with it or a grey crow or the likes.'

As his mother made the Sign of the Cross he hurriedly re-addressed himself to his meal. He realised her interest was thoroughly aroused. Bent over his plate he prepared himself for her next question.

'Is he married?'

'Yes.'

'Has he a family?'

'Eight. Four boys and four girls.'

'May God protect them,' Maggie Conlon whispered and she made the Sign of the Cross a second time. Jim left for work earlier than usual. He needed time to think out a plan of campaign. He wondered how long he could continue with the deception. For the present he would do no more than release minor bulletins concerning the loss of the ear and the effects of same on Fred Rimble. Every weekend Jim Conlon spent most of his time in a neighbourhood tavern. He liked a few drinks and there was the added bonus of a reprieve from the pathological outpourings of his mother. It was here he thought up the idea of providing Fred with a plastic ear.

'You're very thoughtful lately Jim boy,' Matt Weir the publican interrupted his conceptions.

'Friend of mine,' Jim explained, 'took a bad turn lately.'

'Sorry to hear that Jim boy.' Matt Weir patted him on the shoulder and moved off to comfort any other lone birds who might be on the premises.

A week after the accident Maggie took to the bed again. She blamed an old ankle injury which had been aggravated by a sudden change in the weather. Again Jim found himself fending for both of them. Maggie spent three full days in bed and might have spent three weeks had not Jim resorted to his friend Fred Rimble. When he returned for lunch on the third day he found her with the clothes tucked up to her chin. Her head was almost completely muffled by the red flannellette. The martyred look had returned to her face. The room reeked of recently-applied embrocation and every so often there were the old familiar sighs of untold suffering.

'This will be the death of me,' Maggie said. Jim sat silently on the bed and carefully prepared his release.

'God alone knows what I go through,' Maggie groaned.

'Fred Rimble's wife left him.' The announcement was made matter of factly. It took some time before Maggie was able to transfer from herself to this latest development.

'Was there another man?' she asked after a while.

'Afraid so,' Jim said.

'A neighbour I'll warrant.'

'Right first time,' Jim confirmed. 'His best friend to boot.' Wisely Jim arose and left the room. Maggie's next question might prove too much for him. She was on her feet early the following morning. A fine breakfast awaited him when he came downstairs. While he dined Maggie spoke of the perfidy of neighbours. She roundly cursed the ruffian who stole Fred Rimble's wife. Weeks were to pass before she took ill again, this time with nothing more than a crick in the neck. Maggie's cricks, however, were like no other. They might last for weeks or develop into far more sinister aches. Jim roused her by the simple expedient of telling her that Fred Rimble had broken both legs in another car crash. By the time the New Year was due Fred Rimble had, in addition to his earlier mishaps, broken his collar bone, both hands, numerous ribs and to crown his misfortune lost his second ear. It was the removal of the remaining auricle which provided Jim with the happiest Christmas he had spent since childhood. Maggie went around all through the festive period shaking her head and bemoaning the terrible loss. Her Christmas was, however, pain-free.

When he informed her about the second ear Maggie suggested that he contact Fred and invite him and the children to spend Christmas with them.

'No,' Jim had answered sagely. 'I know Fred. He's the sort of man who would want to spend Christmas at home.'

'But who's going to cook the Christmas dinner?'

'No problem there,' Jim informed her. 'The eldest girl is fifteen and then there's a woman nearby who looks in now and then.'

'What woman nearby?' Maggie asked suspiciously.

'Just a neighbour,' Jim replied. Maggie searched his face to see if he was concealing anything. 'She wouldn't be by any chance the missus of the man who went off with Fred's wife?'

'No chance,' Jim assured her. 'Fred isn't that sort.'

'Of course not,' Maggie responded at once, 'that wasn't what I meant.'

Spring came round before she complained again. Normally she would have spent the greater part of January in bed and the remainder muffled up downstairs. Every week or ten days Jim would dole out what

112

he privately termed a Rimble ration. Maggie awaited the titbits eagerly and gobbled up each and every one with relish. In January Jim was obliged to dispose by drowning of the eldest daughter whose name was Cornelia and of the youngest who answered to the name of Trixie. He had good reason for resorting to such extremes. His mother had taken suddenly to the bed one wet afternoon on the grounds that she had undergone a serious heart attack. Even the family doctor who knew her every gambit was perplexed.

'It is just possible,' he confided to Jim, 'that she may have suffered the mildest of coronaries.'

Jim sensed that a broken limb would not be sufficient this time nor indeed the loss of a hand or a leg. Her appetite had been whetted. She now needed stronger meat if a cure were to be effected. For this reason he felt obliged to dispose of Cornelia and Trixie. Maggie had jumped out of bed upon hearing the news, her heart miraculously cured.

'That's one funeral I'm not going to miss,' she announced. Try as he might Jim could not dissuade her. The following morning she rose early and purchased a daily paper. Painstakingly she went through the death notices.

'Rattigan, Remney, Reeves,' she intoned the names solemnly. 'Riley, Romney, Rutledge. There's no Rimble here.'

'I know Fred Rimble,' Jim said. 'Fred hates any sort of a show. The funeral would, of course, be private. That's why it's not in the papers.'

'We'll sent him a telegram then,' Maggie insisted, 'and a letter of sympathy. I'll write it myself.'

'Of course,' Jim agreed. 'I'll sent the telegram this

very morning. You go ahead and write your letter and I'll post it for you during the lunch break.'

At his office in the creamery Jim burned the letter. A week later he typed a reply using a fictitious Dublin address. The letter proved the best tonic Maggie ever received. It kept her out of bed for several weeks. When its effects wore off he did away with the other children pair by pair, the first by food poisoning, the second by a car accident and the third by fire. Indeed Fred Rimble himself had been lucky to escape the conflagration with his life. The last proved to be a wise choice of disposal. Since the family home had been razed to the ground Fred was left without a permanent address.

The deaths of the last two Rimble children had a profound effect on Maggie. She took to attending early morning mass on a regular basis. Regardless of the weather she never once opted out. She enquired daily after Fred but news was scant. He had, it was reported, left the country and taken up work in Australia.

'Too many memories in the home place,' Maggie had observed when Jim informed her of Fred's departure. 'I imagine that if it were me I would do the very same thing,' she said wistfully.

Summer passed. Autumn russetted the leaves and the winds laid them out lovingly on the soft earth. Jim Conlon grew fat and content.

'There's a shine to you lately Jim boy,' Matt Weir told him one night.

Then winter came and inevitably Maggie Conlon took to the bed. In spite of assurances from her own doctor and from a specialist she became convinced that she was suffering from cancer of the throat. She submitted herself to X-rays and to countless other tests. The net result was that there was no evidence whatsoever to show that there was the least trace of the dread disease of which she complained. The weeks passed and when no decline set in she became even more insistent that cancer had taken hold of her windpipe. To prove it she fell back upon a comprehensive repertoire of wheezes, many of them spine-chilling, others weak and pathetic.

The contentment to which Jim Conlon had grown accustomed became a thing of the past. He lost weight. All the old tensions with some new ones in their wake returned to bedevil him. He tried every ruse to rouse his mother but all to no avail. She became so morbid in herself that she made him go for the parish priest every week. When the last rites were administered she would close her eyes as if resigning herself to death. In the end Jim was driven to his wit's end. One night he returned from the pub in what seemed to be a highly agitated state. In reality he was playing the last trump left in his hand.

'I've just had some dreadful news,' he informed his mother.

The lacklustre eyes showed no change nor did she adjust her position in the bed.

'Fred Rimble is dead,' Jim told her. The news had the desired effect. At once she sat upright.

'How did it happen?' she asked after she had crossed herself and begged God's mercy on his soul.

'They say he died of a broken heart,' Jim informed her.

'A broken heart!' she exclaimed tearfully and wondered why she had never thought of this novel way out herself.

115

'That's what they said,' Jim spoke with appropriate sadness.

'Well it's all behind him now the poor man,' Maggie Conlon spoke resignedly. A few days later at Maggie's insistence they had a High Mass said for Fred Rimble in Dirreenroe parish church. It was an unpretentious affair with no more than the three priests, the parish clerk and themselves involved. As soon as they arrived home Maggie prepared lunch and when they had eaten she went at once to her bed vowing that she would never leave it.

'But what's wrong with you?' Jim asked in anguish. 'You were fine ten minutes ago. You put away a feed fit for a ploughman.'

'I know. I know,' she said weakly, 'but the bitter truth is that I think my heart is beginning to break.'

'This beats all,' Jim fumed.

'Now, now,' said Maggie. 'You mustn't let it upset you. It's not in the least like a coronary or angina. There's nothing like the pain. I'll just lie here now and wait for my time to come.'

She closed her eyes and a blissful look settled on her face.

In the tavern Jim sat on his own in a deserted corner. Midway through his third drink Matt Weir came from behind the counter and saluted him. When he didn't answer Matt asked if there was anything wrong.

'Look at me Matt,' Jim spoke despondently. 'Look at me and tell me what you see.'

'I see a friend and a neighbour,' Matt Weir answered.

'No Matt,' Jim countered. 'What you see is a man who killed the best friend he ever had.'

# Death Be Not Proud
## John B. Keane

There are more shades to John B. Keane's humour than there are colours in the rainbow. Wit, pathos, compassion, shrewdness and a glorious sense of fun and roguery are seen in this book. This fascinating exploration of the stiking yet intangible Irish characteristics show us Keane's sensitivity and deep understanding of everyday life in a rural community.

John B. Keane draws our attention to both the comic and tragic effects of small town gossip in 'The Hanging' — a tale of accusation by silence in a small village — and 'The Change' — a carefully etched comment on a town waking up to undiscovered sexuality. With his natural sense of character, a gift for observing and capturing traits he gives us a hilarious, mischievous and accurate portrait of the balance of justice in 'You're on Next Sunday' and 'A Tale of Two Furs'. We see his uncommon gift for creating characters and atmosphere in 'Death Be Not Proud' and 'The Fort Field'.

*Keane's magic, authentic language and recurrent humour weave their spells over the reader making this exciting book a 'must' for all Keane fans.*

# Letters of Successful T.D.
## John B. Keane

This bestseller takes a humourous peep at the correspondence of an Irish parliamentary deputy. Keane's eyes have fastened on the human weaknesses of a man who secured power through the ballot box, and uses it to ensure the comfort of his family and friends.

# Letters of an Irish Parish Priest
## John B. Keane
There is a riot of laughter in every page and its theme is the correspondence between a country parish priest and his nephew who is studying to be a priest. Father O'Mora has been referred to by one of his parishioners as one who 'is suffering from an overdose of racial memory aggravated by religious bigotry.' John B. Keane's humour is neatly pointed, racy of the soil and never forced. This book gives a picture of a way of life which though in great part is vanishing is still familiar to many of our countrymen who still believe 'that priests could turn them into goats'. It brings out all the humour and pathos of Irish life. It is hilariously funny and will entertain and amuse everyone.

# The Gentle Art of Matchmaking
and other important things
## John B. Keane
This book offers a feast of Keane, one of Ireland's best loved playwrights. The title essay reminds us that while some marriages are proverbially made in heaven, others have been made in the back parlour of a celebrated pub in Listowel and none the worse for that! But John B. Keane has other interests besides matchmaking, and these pieces mirror many moods and attitudes. Who could ignore Keane on Potato-Cakes? Keane on skinless sausages? or Half-Doors? Is there a husband alive who will not recognise someone near and dear to him when he reads, with a mixture of affection and horror, the essay Female Painters? And, more seriously, there are other pieces that reflect this writer's deep love of tradition: his nostalgic re-creation of an Irish way of life that is gone forever.

# Unlawful Sex and Other Testy Matters
## John B. Keane

Illicit sex is bad for the heart. I do not say so personally but
it is now widely believed in continental medical circles that
sex without a license will put paid to the beating of the most
consistent ticker. It was also accepted in a limited way by
certain of the religious who, fair play to them, insisted for
starters that it was bad for marriage first and for a number
of other things afterwards. .

A collection of hilarious essays *Unlawful Sex and Other
Testy Matters* deals with all aspects of life in rural Ireland
including 'Things that happen in Bed', 'Young Love',
'Breaking Wind', and 'Skillet Pots'.


# Letters of an Irish Minister of State
## John B. Keane

Every person who has read John B. Keane's bestseller
*Letters of a Successful T.D.* will be familiar with the exploits
of Tull MacAdoo who was a rural backbencher. In this
book he becomes Minister for Bogland Areas with Special
Responsibility for Game and Wildlife. He is a powerful,
resourceful and cunning man who can get things done for
his 'Number Ones' by 'using every trick in the book and
some not in the book'. The reader will chuckle to himself as
he enters the web of local intrigue and petty skullduggery
among the rural politicians.

We also meet Tull's family: his spendthrift son, Mick, at
university who will make Tull the laughing stock of the con-
stituency if he fails his exams again, his narrow-minded,
martyred, hypochondriac wife who 'suffers from head to
toe', and his best-loved child, Kate, in whom he confides his
problems. There is also Tull's running feud with James
Flannery, the local N.T. Although Tull is a little on the
ignorant side he has learned his lessons in the Dail and deals
with his opponent not in the most lawful way but in very
effective ways.

# Letters of a Matchmaker
## John B. Keane
These are the letters of a country matchmaker faithfully recorded by John B. Keane, whose knowledge of matchmaking is second to none.

In these letters is revealed the unquenchable, insatiable longing that smoulders unseen under the mute, impassive faces of our bachelor brethren.

Comparisons may be odious but readers will find it fascinating to contrast the Irish matchmaking system with that of the 'Cumangettum Love Parlour' in Philadelphia. They will meet many unique characters from the Judas Jennies of New York to Fionnuala Crust of Coomasahara who buried two giant-sized husbands but eventually found happiness with a pint-sized jockey from North Cork.


# Letters of a Love-Hungry Farmer
## John B. Keane
John B. Keane has introduced a new word into the English language — *chastitute*. This is the story of a chastitute, i.e. a man who has never lain down with a woman for reasons which are fully disclosed within this book. It is the tale of a lonely man who will not humble himself to achieve his heart's desire, whose need for female companionship whines and whimpers throughout. Here are the hilarious sex excapades of John Bosco McLane culminating finally in one dreadful deed.